THE ACCUSATION

BANDI is the Korean word for firefly – a light that shines in the darkness. It is the pseudonym of an anonymous dissident writer still living in his homeland of North Korea.

DEBORAH SMITH is the Man Booker International Prize-winning translator of *The Vegetarian* by Han Kang and other books.

THE ACCUSATION

FORBIDDEN STORIES FROM INSIDE NORTH KOREA

BANDI

This book has been selected to receive financial assistance from English PEN's PEN Translates programme, supported by Arts Council England. English PEN exists to promote literature and our understanding of it, to uphold writers' freedoms around the world, to campaign against the persecution and imprisonment of writers for stating their views, and to promote the friendly co-operation of writers and the free exchange of ideas.
www.englishpen.org

Supported using public funding by

ARTS COUNCIL
ENGLAND

This paperback edition published in 2018

First published in Great Britain in 2017 by Serpent's Tail,
an imprint of Profile Books Ltd
3 Holford Yard
Bevin Way
London
WCIX 9HD
www.serpentstail.com

Original title: 고발 / Gobal
First published in Korea by Chogabje.com

Copyright © 2014, 2018 by Bandi and Happy Unification Road
Translation copyright © 2017, 2018 by Deborah Smith

1 3 5 7 9 10 8 6 4 2

Printed and bound by CPI Group (UK) Ltd, Croydon CR0 4YY

The moral right of the author has been asserted.

A CIP record for this book can
be obtained from the British Library

ISBN 978 1 78125 755 5
eISBN 978 1 78283 312 3

Mixed Sources
Product group from well-managed
forests and other controlled sources
www.fsc.org Cert no. TT-COC-002227
© 1996 Forest Stewardship Council
FSC

Contents

NOTE FROM THE PUBLISHER

The provenance of the Korean manuscript from which this translation is derived is detailed in the two afterwords to this edition. In order to protect the identity of the author, some of those details have been changed. Beyond the assessment presented there, the publishers have no further information about the origins of *The Accusation*, but believe it to be an important work of North Korean samizdat literature and a unique portrayal of life under a totalitarian dictatorship.

In Place of a Preface

[A poem included with the original manuscript
of *The Accusation*, with this title]

That old man of Europe with his bristling beard
Claimed that capitalism is a pitch-black realm
While communism is a world of light.

I, Bandi, of this so-called world of light,
Fated to shine only in a world of darkness,
Denounce in front of the whole world
That light which is truly fathomless darkness,
Black as a moonless night at the year's end.

—Bandi

Record of a Defection

Sangki, it's me, Il-cheol. I'm sitting down now to write this record of my defection. You remember Choi Seo-hae's *Record of an Escape*, which he wrote back in 1920? But now it's 1990, more than fifty years since our land was liberated from the Japanese colonizers—and unlike Choi, I'm escaping from my own country. Sounds absurd, doesn't it? But I want you to understand, so I'll try to explain it all as simply as possible. In a way, you could say it all began with a medicine packet, the one I showed you that time.

The packet fell into my hands quite by chance. You remember my brother's youngest son—he was eight years old then. The kid used to be at our place so often you'd think we were his parents. Of course, this wasn't so strange when you consider that the apartment I shared with my wife was practically next to my brother's house, where I'd lived until I got married. But as I think back on it now, that wasn't the

1

only reason for the visits. No, the real reason was my wife's constant readiness to drop whatever she was doing and lavish attention on the kid. She was tenderhearted by nature, true, but this was something else—she welled up with compassion every time she set eyes on him, and was always happy to have him stay over, unrolling an extra mattress right by hers.

After a while I got to thinking that perhaps the maternal instinct grows even stronger when a woman doesn't have a child of her own, making the most of whatever outlet it has. In her eyes the boy could do no wrong, and he adored her every bit as much. The day everything changed, the day of the medicine packet incident, was also the first time he showed up at our door.

My wife had gone downstairs to help our local Party secretary repaper his ceiling, leaving me to my own devices. I was getting on with some work when the kid burst in, looked around for his aunt, and, when he couldn't find her, promptly settled on pestering me instead. It was a kite he was after; we were at the end of autumn, when the wind which tosses the fallen leaves starts producing the kind of splendid gusts that children find irresistible. And my nephew was so innocently eager, I didn't have it in my heart to disappoint him.

Now, for a kite, ordinary paper wouldn't do—you needed something tough yet pliable—and I remembered there'd been some scraps left over from when we'd last repapered the door. As it was, I ended up turning the place upside down looking for them, even rummaging through the wardrobe where we stored the bedding during the day. But when I thrust my hand into the tiny gap between the quilts and the back of the wardrobe, the rustling material my fingers closed around wasn't the offcuts from the door, but a paper packet of loose pills.

I didn't think much of it at first, just carried on with my search, but I soon found my thoughts straying back to it. Where was my wife in all this? The more I wondered about those pills, the more puzzling they appeared. What kind of medicine has to be hidden away out of sight like this, and taken only when nobody's looking? What kind of illness has no external symptoms? Then it dawned on me. Of course—it had to be something to keep her from getting pregnant!

I was too distracted to make a good job of the kite, and I cut myself twice in the process of making it. The more I thought about it, the less likely it seemed that confronting my wife directly would get me a straight answer. And so I tried a different tack, and ended up knocking on your door, Sangki, seeking your advice as a doctor. But what you told me when you looked at the pills I'd brought only served to confirm my worst suspicions.

"Contraceptives?" I burst out, forgetting the many other patients, some women included, who were waiting just outside your consulting room. "Are you sure?"

"Now, now, there's no need," you blustered, wincing at the volume of my voice, your eyes entreating me to remember where we were. I left you standing there and raced back home, not even stopping for breath, the accusation balanced on my tongue like a primed grenade the whole way. But when I finally did fling our door open, I found myself face-to- face with my

3

wife—and the pin jammed. Seeing her there reminded me that this was a delicate situation, one in which I'd do best to tread carefully. After all, it was an open secret that my wife and I weren't exactly equals.

I'm not talking about any difference in personality—there was nothing much to choose between us there—but as far as our family history was concerned we couldn't have been further apart, and that, after all, is what counts in this society. On her side, my wife could boast a spotless record, without even so much as a distant relation whose loyalty to the Party might be questionable. Whereas on my side, a different story . . . I've no doubt more than a few jaws would have hit the ground when word got out that Lee Il-cheol and Nam Myung-ok were engaged. "A white heron and a black crow—what good can come of a match like that?" Those would have been the words on everyone's lips.

And now that white heron had been going behind my back, looking out for her own interests at the expense of our marriage, which after all was the one blemish on her otherwise flawless reputation. This was the first thought that sprang to mind, and was it really any wonder? How else could I interpret the fact that my wife, for whom married life should hardly have had time to lose its shine, wished to avoid having a baby with me?

"What's happened?" my wife asked, seeing my mood as soon as I rushed in.

I ground my teeth to give my mouth something to do, cracked my fingers, then threw myself down on the bench by the window, still panting from the exertion. Carefully releasing a gentle breath, my wife picked up a pack of cigarettes and a matchbox, walked over to the bench, and set them down on the windowsill. But I wasn't about to be placated by this show of wifely consideration. The whole incident had forced me to remember the one thing I didn't want to think about, the one thing I could never get away from—my "standing." And the reason mine was so low? Because my father was a murderer—albeit only an accidental one, and one whose sole victim was a crate of rice seedlings.

This was just after the war, when the socialist system of cooperative farming had only recently been introduced. In other words, it was a time of great upheaval, one of history's so-called transitional periods, so surely it was a matter of course that the majority would find themselves out of their depth. Using greenhouses to raise rice seedlings was utterly alien to those who worked the land. For farmers who'd never known any other way of cultivating rice than to grow the seedlings in water-filled containers before transplanting them into the paddy fields, this new method was bound to prove tricky at first.

And that was how my father came to make his terrible mistake, the mistake that was to see him branded an "anti-Party, antirevolutionary element," a black mark that appeared overnight but that would dog our family for generations.

There was also the matter of his land, a scant few acres which he'd carved out for himself before liberation, all through his own blood and sweat, and which, when collectivization began, he hadn't relinquished as meekly as he might have. In this, he was like the child of a second wife, whose position in the household is already so precarious that it needs only the slightest trip to topple over into disaster. Ultimately, he was arrested, hauled off to a place whose location we would never know, while we, his wife and children, were turned out of our home, where we'd often been able to sate our hunger by simply reaching up to pluck a ripe persimmon, and sent on forced "migration" to this barren, unfamiliar land, so close to the border with China that the clamor of the Yalu's rapids seemed constantly in our ears.

When the narrator of Choï's *Record of an Escape* has to make his way through the badlands around the Tumen River, a region bearing the distant memory of marauding Manchu tribes, he and his family still manage to maintain a spark of hope, unquenched even in the midst of adversity. But for my mother, who'd crossed the Gaema pass with her two young sons after seeing her husband taken away in handcuffs, there was only a heavy shroud of helplessness and desolation, with not a single strand of hope woven into its weft.

The people in Choï's book were fortunate in a way, heading into that adversity of their own free will, with nothing but their determination driving them on. They certainly seemed fortunate compared with us, being forcibly wrenched from everything that familiarity had made dear to us and "migrating" under armed guard to these distant parts where both the shape of the mountains and the sound of the water were foreign.

It was among these strange, comfortless sights that my mother breathed her last, still young, but beaten down by suffering and resentment. Her eyes were staring open when she died, her children's prospective future pricking her heart like one of the thick icicles that were abundant in our new home.

And now what fresh tragedy is unfolding for my mother's vengeful spirit to howl at. Sangki! When I couldn't remain sitting in our apartment any longer I jumped up from the window seat and fled, still with the packet of contraceptives stuffed in my pocket. To my mother's grave, to the foot of the Gaema pass—even I can't remember everywhere my feet carried me that day, my upcoming shift far from my mind, until it was late in the evening and I found myself back at home. I can only recall that my wife greeted me exactly as usual, and took care to set each dish down within reach of my spoon and chopsticks. In other words, she showed me no less affection than she always did, though I repaid her with sharp scrutiny. She was unchanged in every respect, from her gaze, which seemed shyly aware of the warmth that suffused it, down to her soft voice and gestures. If anything, these characteristics seemed to intensify as the days went by. But this only served to increase my anxiety. It wouldn't be the last time that one suspicion gave birth to another and odd rumors came to my ears.

I mean the rumor about the steam that rose from our third-floor apartment, once early in the morning and then again a few hours later—twice in the same day, without fail, which could only mean two rounds of cooking. Apartment

7

living makes it all too easy to keep an eye on other people's business, and though I was aware that such rumors are unlikely to be entirely groundless, I hadn't risen to the bait; I didn't want my wife to become the victim of women's vicious tongues. Several days later, though, something happened that meant I could no longer turn a blind eye.

I was overseeing a welding job that had me perched on the arm of a hundred-ton crane from the very start of the day, with an uninterrupted view of the area around the factory. Sure enough, I saw that second round of steam spurt out of our chimney, a good few hours after I myself had had breakfast and left for work. Winter had already set in and it was bitingly cold, but I climbed up onto the crane's arm the next day and the day after that, on the pretext of making sure that the welding was proceeding safely. Only on the third day did I clamber down not long after I'd gone up, make a plausible excuse to the foreman, and hurry straight home.

"Oh! What are you doing home?"

I'd surprised my wife in the kitchen, and she'd cried out before she had time to think. The whole place was a fug of condensation, owing to the steam belching out of a large pot on the stove. My wife forced a brittle smile, which sat awkwardly on her usually open features.

"I went out without my tape measure," I said, looking suitably shamefaced.

"Your tape measure? And they sent you back for a thing as small as that?"

Taking it rather too much to heart, as though it were her fault I'd had to come back from the factory, she hurried away to fetch it. Seeing my chance, I lifted the lid of the pot and peered inside, impatient to have the riddle solved—but all I saw was an insipid mess of dog food: a scant handful of corn and some grains of rice jumbled up with dried radish leaves that no human could have got any nourishment from. So my wife was feeding dogs!

I wasn't quick enough fitting the lid back on; I still had my hand on it when my wife returned with the tape measure.

"What are you doing?" she said, alarmed.

"What about you?" I countered. "Why are you bothering with dog food?"

"What? Oh, yes, for dogs, that's right . . . because . . ."

"You make this every day?"

"Yes. I . . . Well, please just concentrate on your work. Don't worry yourself about household affairs. And try not to make this kind of mistake again," she said, pressing the tape measure into my hand. "The Party secretary from downstairs came around yesterday. He's promised to seriously consider the possibility of you joining the Party, and he asked me to give you my full support in the meantime, so you don't have anything distracting you from your work. My full support . . ."

She bit down on her lower lip, both eyes brimming, as though the words she was suppressing were threatening to burst forth as tears. She bowed her head, trying to save me from having to witness this show of emotion, but it was still

9

too uncomfortable for me to stay there for a single second longer.

I didn't so much as look at the tape measure, never mind use it in my work, and though it stayed tucked away in my pocket I felt it there like a lead weight. But the strange thing was that from that day onward the cares that had been weighing on me gradually lifted. I reproached myself for having been so underhanded, and began to convince myself that my wife couldn't possibly be using contraceptives for the reason I'd supposed. If it was true that she feared mingling her bloodline with that of a "crow," feared seeing her children tarred with the brush of a Party traitor, the generous affection she'd always shown me would have been nothing but a mask, and that simply wasn't something I was prepared to believe. If I even dared to doubt that woman, I felt, I'd deserve to be struck down. My only wish was for everything to be revealed as a misunderstanding, and for my wife to remain as she had always been, a generous and loving companion.

Time went by without incident, and I was happy to let it do so. Our nephew continued his frequent visits, and our chimney continued to release two rounds of steam each morning, for me now merely a source of gentle self-recrimination. The one noticeable difference was that my wife was increasingly anxious to have our nephew stay over. She claimed she had trouble falling asleep on those nights when I had to stay late at the factory, though this had never been the case before.

It was on one such night, a month ago now, that things finally came to a head—the reason I started to write this record.

As my wife cleared away the dishes from the evening meal, she reminded me several times to drop by my brother's on my way to the factory the next day and to send our nephew over. This was nothing unusual in itself, but on that particular day I wasn't able to fulfill her request. I did stop off at my brother's, but my sister-in-law informed me that the boy had already gone out with his father, to look for old traction cables. Despite his punishing work in the coal mines, my brother snatched every opportunity to go out scavenging for scrap metal, which he then turned into kitchen utensils to trade for extra rations.

It just so happened that this was one of those times when the evening shift finished earlier than expected. This was quite frequently the case, as the tasks assigned to my work detail, which was in charge of developing and implementing new technologies, were rarely planned out in advance, and this made scheduling tricky. Conscious that my wife would be missing our nephew, I took care not to dawdle on the way home.

Just after midnight, the interior of our building was quiet and still. I went up the stairs two at a time, past the second floor where the local Party secretary lived, to the third and highest floor, where my wife should have been asleep. But when I stepped into the corridor I could see light still seeping out through the chink at the bottom of our door.

Still awake? I thought. *She really must be missing our nephew.* I recalled the plaintive tone in which she'd asked me to send him over, and felt even more sorry for letting her

11

down. I went to open the door; it didn't budge, but the light seeping out at the bottom abruptly died. My wife must have finally decided to try to get some sleep. I tried the handle again, but the door was latched on the inside. I knocked. There was no response. "It's me," I called out, rapping on the door again. In a flash, the light revived. I heard what seemed like our kitchen door swinging open, but there was still neither sight nor sound of my wife. "It's me!" I called again.

Only then did I hear her quick soft footsteps, and a muffled apology as she opened the door.

"Hadn't you gone to bed yet?"

"I've had a few things to get on with."

Sangki!

How could I have imagined that a dark shadow was lurking behind the very door I stepped through then? My wife began to lay out the bedding and I slowly tugged off my work clothes. And that was when I heard it—our front door opening, then closing, the sound unmistakable. I whipped around and instinctively dashed out in pursuit. Footsteps descending the stairs, quick and soft, clearly belonging to someone who knew his way even in the dark. I clattered down after them, then jerked to a halt. There were too many thoughts whirling in my head.

So this was the answer to all the riddles. But if this was the case, what was to be gained by laying hands on the culprit? As I turned and retraced my steps, I felt the blood run backward through my veins.

I was expecting to find my wife in a state, but not one as extreme as what confronted me when I marched in through the open door. She was collapsed in a corner of the room, sobbing with her face turned to the wall.

"Stop crying!" I burst out, planted like a stake in the middle of the room.

"Minsu's uncle!" she cried.

My wife struggled to her knees, raising her head to reveal a mask of tears. I'd used to like the way she referred to me using our nephew's name—it felt intimate, preparation for the day when we'd have a child of our own and I'd be "So-and-so's father." In that moment, though, it seemed a slap in the face, a sharp reminder of where I ranked in her affections.

"Minsu's uncle, is it? Well, if that's how you want it, that's how it'll be. A husband's clearly not worth your while!"

"Minsu's uncle! That's not it."

"Shut up." Gasping with fury, I jerked the bookstand away from the wall, retrieved the packet of contraceptives I'd hidden there, and hurled them at my wife's feet.

I was on the point of losing my sense of reason.

"And I suppose this isn't what it seems either? Why are you taking them? Afraid of getting a mongrel? By who? Who is he? Out with it!"

I seized hold of my wife's slumped shoulders and hauled her to her feet, but she gripped my upper arms and began to shriek, her voice juddering with sobs.

"You mustn't, you mustn't, you mustn't ask me that. . . ."

If she hadn't released her grip and staggered hastily in the direction of the clothes chest, I wouldn't have been responsible for my actions.

Muttering "You mustn't, you mustn't" like someone who had taken leave of her senses, she fumbled with the lid of the box. She lifted it, reached inside, and brought out a notebook from beneath the pile of clothes. She dragged her feet as she walked back to me, clutching the notebook as though this was the last card she had left to play.

"What's this?"

I snatched the notebook from her. Inside there were dated entries—a diary.

"You must believe me, I didn't know he was here. . . . He must have sneaked in while I was in the bathroom. . . . I swear I haven't deceived you, I swear." My wife collapsed in a heap once more, and her shoulders resumed their violent quaking.

Only then did I recognize the signs in front of me: my wife's disheveled hair, the loose thread hanging from the front of her jacket where a button had been torn off. She had clearly been in some fierce, desperate struggle. The blood that had been thrumming through my veins seemed to quiet down, leaving me able to think more clearly, my wife's cries now little more than background noise. My gaze darted back to the diary, hanging open in my hand.

4th December

He was here again today. I remind myself that he's looking out for my husband's interests, but as grateful as I am, his visits are starting to bother me. Especially now when these visits seem to happen every time my husband's out of the house. But it's not just that—each time he shows up, his manner is slightly different from what it was before. Surely a man over forty would never think of me that way . . . but I wish I could be certain!

What am I to do? I'm afraid that if I start discouraging him by behaving coldly, things will go badly for my husband, but I'm afraid that if I don't . . . Well, never mind all that. What does it matter if there's some minor trouble for me? Even death wouldn't be too much to bear if it meant my husband was allowed to join the Party. . . .

Sangki!

That night, I stayed standing in the middle of the room for the whole time it took me to read that diary, from the first to the very last page. This diary in which my wife had recorded two years' worth of incidents and feelings, albeit frequently skipping days. I didn't simply read this diary; it hauled my gaze across its pages, my mind on a knife-edge, so that even granting the speed with which I raced through it, the words felt imprinted on my memory, like a photograph. Some entries follow:

13th March

A message came from the local Party secretary, saying that my husband would be too busy to leave the factory today so I should bring him his lunch at work. And so I ended up revisiting the technology innovation department, my husband's current place of work and my own former one, for the first time in a very long while.

Just as the name suggests, the department deals with developing and testing new tools and techniques to improve factory production. It's a small place, set a little apart from the main building, and with only a handful of permanent staff. Min-hyuk happened to be with me when I received the message, so I brought him with me to see his uncle.

Though it's been only six months since I got married and stopped working, each familiar sight brought a smile to my face. The corrugated red roof, which used to shimmer with heat haze even in the winter, so long as the weather was mild; the little prep room that looked like a matchbox stuck onto the side of the building; its tiny, blue-framed window, where the weeping willow's trailing limbs used to dance in the breeze through every season, sending me into a daydream just like a silly schoolgirl; my desk, its sloping surface recalling the ones we used to have at school, where I sat and sketched out technical drawings or drafted models—everything was just as I remembered. The desk happened to be vacant just then, so I sat down. There in that spot, the joy of getting to know my future husband, the sorrow of getting to know him better, flooded back as intense as when they'd first swept over me.

That unforgettable day when I, a young woman fresh out of mechanic school, first sat in front of that desk! That day, as all days, the name Lee Il-cheol attracted my notice, when I glimpsed it through the willow branches swaying just outside my window, on the bulletin board that stood in the yard. As I read on with mounting surprise, the title of the bulletin—'Comrade Lee Il-cheol, Inventor! Further success in new inventions: the automatic plane!'—reminded me of a poster from middle school: "Great talent plus great effort! Student Lee Il-cheol's Study Experience," further ensuring that the name lodged in my mind. . . .

There I was on my very first job, a colleague of the senior I'd held in such esteem, who had always seemed so far above me! I was so delighted by this lucky chance, and so proud to be working shoulder to shoulder with such an upstanding young man, that the desk I sat at felt like an old friend, and the willow outside the window seemed to dance for sheer joy.

To think how swiftly that happiness vanished! I hadn't been there long when, one day toward the end of the afternoon, an announcement was made. All Party members were to stay behind that evening, as the Party cell secretary had an important matter to discuss.

When I laid down my tools and headed to the break room for the meeting, how shocked I was to see the brilliant inventor, head lowered and shoulders slumped, trudging out through the main door! That young man—whose formal education had stopped at middle school, yet whose unflagging program of self-study had left him with greater intelligence and skill than any college graduate; who, like the legendary creature with the head of a dragon and the body of a horse, outstripped everyone else in both brains and brawn—how could anything of importance be discussed without him?

But such meetings were called quite often, and each time saw the "inventor" turned out of the break room with his tail between his legs! Why was I so affected by this contemptuous treatment? Why, when I found out that he had been unable to attend college, as his poor standing prevented him from joining the Party, did I find myself imagining how both the middle-school poster and the recent bulletin must seem meaningless imitations to him, mere children's toys compared with the real thing? My sympathy was so great, I even began to feel a vague, indeterminate hatred on his behalf. But this hatred was mingled with a far more tender feeling toward the inventor himself, that young man with the burning eyes, so humble and diligent despite his extraordinary mind. . . .

People write books and sing songs claiming that love is this or that. But to me, love was indistinguishable from sympathy. That intolerable fretfulness at your inability to take any of the suffering on yourself, that irrepressible impulse to offer up your own flesh as a sacrifice, anything to bring some measure of relief . . .

In just such a blaze of sympathy, love budded within me and burst into glorious flower. While I sat immobile at my old desk, letting my mind slide back into bygone days, Min-hyuk went haring around the workshop, darting into and out of the break room as though it was all his private domain. He even came out with a shrill little song about how his uncle was number one here, so he had the right to do as he pleased. . . .

Seeing Min-hyuk in such high spirits, blithely unaware of the reality of the situation, threw his uncle's misfortune

18

into sharper relief. My eyes grew misty at the thought of him having to go through life as a gemstone scuffed by ignorant feet. Oh, when would Min-hyuk's uncle join the Party and see his true worth discovered?

23rd April

It was late afternoon, and I was busy mending my husband's work clothes when Min-hyuk burst into the apartment. He was sobbing so violently he could barely speak, and his cheeks were streaked with grubby marks.

"What's all this, hey?"

"I-I c-can't be class president anymore."

"What? Why not?"

"The t-teacher s-said so. . . ."

"But why?"

"D-don't knoow."

With great difficulty I managed to calm Min-hyuk down and dry his tears, but there was no chance of carrying on with my sewing. He still had his satchel with him, I noticed, meaning he'd come straight here from school. No doubt he expected that I would be able to solve this problem with a click of my fingers. His confidence in me was a heavy burden.

For my own family, I could boast nothing better than a father who was a member of the municipal administration board, but Min-hyuk's parents held even this lowly position in high esteem. The boy had clearly picked up on this, hence his coming to me before his parents. The tears might have stopped streaming down his face but they were still there in his eyes, dark shining eyes like those of a young calf. It was impossible for me to do nothing. Instructing Min-hyuk to stay and amuse himself, I went straight to the people's school. As chance would have it, the supervisor of the senior years—the Boy Scouts—was none other than Moon Yeong-hee, a childhood friend I'd lost touch with. Seeing her, I figured this would be easier than I'd thought. But as soon as she'd heard what I had to say, I realized that this was far more serious than a snub from some snot-nosed kid.

"There's no secrets between us," she began, "so I'll tell you very frankly how things stand. This is an issue that comes up time and again once the children become Boy Scouts. I received a proposal from their homeroom teacher to give your nephew the post of class president. His grades were already at the top, and his comportment was first-class. But when I went to get the proposal ratified by the Party secretary, I got, 'Comrade, don't you know that this child's father was deported to Wonsan?' and, well, that was that. The Boy Scouts are the first level in the Party hierarchy, so we simply can't use the same criteria as we did when the children were younger."

Moon Yeong-hee's words left me utterly dumbfounded. Even if I could have thought of something to say, I doubt I would have been capable of producing the words.

"But I had no idea you were the boy's aunt. With a standing like yours, how—"

"That's all done with," I broke in sharply, cutting Moon Yeong-hee off in mid-flow. Now that I'd found my tongue again, I thought I might as well make use of it. "I know you've told me all this only as a kindness, and I'm grateful for your friendship, truly I am. I'd never ask for this favor otherwise. Your husband works in the citizens' registration department, doesn't he? Could you ask him to get me a copy of the file on my husband's family?" Of course, I was well aware of their standing, but my shock that a case of rotten roots could affect even such a young bud as Min-hyuk forced me to take this risk.

Though Moon Yeong-hee promised to do what she could, I walked out of the schoolyard with faltering steps.

30th April

Some days it seems life is just a never-ending obstacle course. Each day brings some new setback, tying my stomach in knots. Today's was meeting Seon-hee at the ration center. Two years my senior at middle school and a former classmate of my husband's, she'd always treated me with the utmost kindness. The center was so crowded, we had to wait outside for over an hour after we'd received our coupons. We'd just been standing there chatting about this and that when she asked me a question out of the blue.

"Has he paid a visit to your apartment?"

"Who?"

"You know, Jang-hyuk, one of the three from our school who went to study abroad."

"Ah, him. The judge's son . . ."

"That's right, that's right. Him."

"How is he?

"You mean he still hasn't been to see your husband?"

"Oh, I . . . I'm not sure. . . ."

"Well, he looked pretty much the same at the alumni gathering. It was just a few days ago, right after he got back. At my house." Seon-hee frowned at me.

"What is it?"

"Before we sat down to eat someone asked why Comrade Il-cheol wasn't there, and Jang-hyuk said Il-cheol was away visiting relatives so he'd decided to visit him separately."

If my ration center number hadn't been called just then, I'm not sure how I would have kept my composure. As it was, I rushed in to the counter with only the barest of nods to Seon-hee, a riot of thoughts drumming in my head. If this Jang-hyuk didn't want to associate with someone of my husband's standing, why couldn't he just admit it? Why did he have to tell such a stupid lie? It was bad enough that my husband had to deal with mean-spirited contempt, but to ostracize him like that was something else—as though Jang-hyuk genuinely feared contamination. It was all too sad for words.

9th May

I was on my way home with the noodles I'd ordered when a child came up behind me and grabbed my hand. Turning, I saw that it was Jeong-ho, who lived in the same building as Min-hyuk.

"Min-hyuk's crying," the boy told me.

"Oh? Where is he?"

"There, there under that tree."

With the noodles balanced on my head, I let the boy pull me along, ducking into an alley with a barbershop on the corner. Bright green leaves had just begun to sprout from the tree by the side of the road, and Min-hyuk was indeed standing there beneath them. He was leaning against the trunk and staring blankly into the distance, not crying now at least but certainly seeming to have something on his mind.

"Min-hyuk! What's the matter?"

No sooner was the question out of my mouth than Min-hyuk started to sniffle. Jeong-ho answered for him.

"We've just come from school. Min-hyuk crossed the stone bridge first, and some kid said, 'That brat crossed the bridge first, who does he think he is?'"

"And you're just standing here crying about it?" I scolded Min-hyuk. "Jeong-ho, who's the one that called him a brat? Some big bully?"

"Pfft . . . Min-hyuk could swat him like a fly!"

"Then why didn't he? Instead of crying like a dummy."

"As if! That kid's father is a Party officer!"

Jeong-ho's words slid in like a thorn. Clearly, the unspoken thought behind them—*and Min-hyuk's is a traitor*—was also what lay behind the emptiness in Min-hyuk's eyes.

So, Min-hyuk has already begun to bow to the weight of his family circumstances? This early? The moment this thought struck me, I pulled him into a tight embrace. If only I could melt the frost that was chilling his young heart!

Min-hyuk began to cry again, and this time I cried with him.

15th May

Today I bumped into the head of the factory's technology innovation department. Ever since my first day working there, making technical drawings under his supervision, he'd treated me like his own daughter. But this man who, on any other day, would have greeted me with a friendly word and a smile before passing on casually down the street, stopped in his tracks and addressed me with a sharp "Well now!"

I stopped too, both confused and alarmed by his tone.

"You remember the publisher, the one specializing in science and technology, that I sent around to your apartment a while ago?"

"Yes, he came to talk with Min-hyuk's uncle. . . ."

"Right, that's what I'm talking about. How did the residents' officer come to hear of it? From you?"

"Why would I have told them? It was just a visit. . . ."

"Well, the factory officer is certainly aware—he even cross-examined me about it. Said he ought to be informed if an outsider was coming to visit the factory, and certainly before the residents' officer, otherwise he'd be put in an embarrassing position."

"Honestly, it had nothing to do with me. I'm sure I'd remember if I'd said something. "

"No, I didn't think you would have. Hmm! He heard about it from somewhere, that's for sure. Pestering me with his silly demands! But I wanted to ask you just in case."

Shaking his head, he continued on his way. But my feet weren't so ready to carry me away—I was beginning to get an inkling of what might have happened. Two days ago, my husband had just finished his lunch and gone out when the publisher knocked on our door, so I'd had to direct him to the factory instead. I didn't accompany him, just told him the way, so the only person who could possibly have seen us was the woman from No. 4, who'd come out to dispose of her coal cinders while we were standing in the corridor. Later that day, though, there'd been another knock on my door.

"Ah . . . Min-hyuk's aunt!" It was the head of the residents' association, who lived downstairs. "You know, you really ought to hurry up and have a child of your own, so I know what to call you!"

She usually enjoyed having the rest of us stand on ceremony, so this casual familiarity threw me at first. As she chatted away about nothing in particular, a broad smile on her face the whole time, I'd just begun to relax when she slipped it in.

"By the way, your family wasn't one of those assigned dirt collection duties this month, was it?"

"Yes, we were."

"Goodness! I never . . ." She failed to muffle a snicker as she jotted something down in her notebook. "But how is

25

it that Min-hyuk's uncle gets such upstanding visitors? Like the one today, for instance. In the dark glasses."

"I don't know what you mean. . . . He was only someone from a publishing house, who wanted to know about the new technologies being developed at the factory." I answered unthinkingly, too busy wondering how she could possibly have seen us. Thinking back now, she must have heard the gossip from the woman at No. 4, come to me to verify it, then reported it to the residents' police. All of which could mean only one thing: Our apartment was under daily observation.

How, how could this be? Even if the father had committed such a heinous crime that it really did warrant his death, what kind of crime could belong to his sons, who had been mere children at the time? And even if someone had decided that it was right and proper for the sons to bear the blame, how could it possibly be right for Min-hyuk to have his life darkened by the shadow of his grandfather, a man he'd never even set eyes on? No, it was too much. Too much, truly, for innocent people whose lives consisted of doing as they were told. If Min-hyuk's uncle found out we were under surveillance, the shame and anger would cripple him. How could he bear to show his face after that? He'd feel as exposed as if his socks were inside out!

What could I do? One thing was certain: My husband would have to be kept in the dark. But what if that wasn't possible? The prospect of him finding out was already making me nervous.

23rd May

Less than a month after our meeting at the school, Moon Yeong-hee brought the file I'd asked for. And now I almost wished she hadn't, that I'd never set eyes on the terrible thing. Whatever possessed me, to make me ask for it?

> Lee Il-cheol
> Family: Class 149
> Evaluation: hostile element
> Father: Lee Myeong-su
>> As a prosperous farmer under the Japanese colonizers, harbored resentment toward the Party's agricultural collectivization policy, and deliberately sabotaged the project to grow rice in greenhouses, in village xx, district xx, Wonsan. Punished as an anti-Party, antirevolutionary element.
> Mother: Jeong In-suk
>> Died at her new place of residence, from resentment toward her husband's punishment.

I stood there with the document clutched in my trembling hand as those bloodthirsty phrases swam in front of my eyes, tangled together into an ugly whirl—"Class 149"; "hostile element"; "anti-Party"; "antirevolutionary." Moon Yeong-hee waited patiently for a while, then gently took the document from me.

"You know, if anyone ever found out that my husband and I smuggled this file out for you, the verdict would be

27

just the same—Class 149. It means the Party considers you a traitor. Our whole family would be deported according to Government Resolution 149, and persecuted for generations."

Class 149! I cringed to hear it spoken out loud. Those words were enough to strike terror into any listener. Even the seal used to stamp the document seemed not some innocuous wax stick but an iron brand, heated in flames and seared indelibly onto the rumps of livestock. It had been used to brand slaves too, in the old days; now Min-hyuk's father and uncle, even young Min-hyuk itself, bore its mark. Not merely on the skin, but biting deep into the flesh.

I'd hoped Moon Yeong-hee might be able to make things easier for Min-hyuk. No such hope was left now. My mind was crowded with threatening clouds, packed so close that not even a pinprick of sunshine could break through. But there was something else—the tear-streaked mess of Min-hyuk's face when he'd come to ask my help that day, and later, leaning against the tree, the empty look in his eyes that belied his young age. I could see his face as though he were there in front of me, only this time the bridge of his nose had been seared with that hideous brand. His father and uncle might have a hard lot in life, but that was nothing compared with this. A blameless child with his whole life already mapped out, forced to follow in his parents' footsteps, step by stumbling step, along that same route of blood and tears.

Involuntarily, the hand that had clutched the document was drawn to my stomach. After all this time of waiting, a new life was finally growing inside me. What a stroke of luck it seemed, now, that I'd been too shy to tell my husband yet. In this country, a mother has only one wish when she brings children into the world: that their passage through life will be blessed. But if she knew for a fact that what lay in wait was an endless path of thorns? She'd need the cruelty of a hardened criminal to condemn a child to that.

Soon, tomorrow at the latest, I'll have to go to the gynecologist.

28th October

Time truly does fly by. The blaze of autumn leaves has vanished from the streets, replaced by a wind rasping through bare branches. The air's vicious chill turns my fretful mind to Min-hyuk. Did he wrap up warmly when he went to school this morning? Every day he looks more and more pitiful, though I don't know why. As though he were some motherless wretch. If he comes back from school with his little face red from cold again, I'll stop whatever I'm doing and rush to embrace him. When I can hold him in my arms, I fancy that the heat of my body can somehow ease his pain, and the pain of that whole unhappy family. Nothing else warms my own heart as much.

If only the local secretary could help my husband to join the Party! And after that, perhaps even Min-hyuk's father . . . Then that stamp of loyalty and honorability would erase the cattle brand. Min-hyuk would never again suffer the scorn of those who feel themselves superior, and our family

29

would no longer be seen through the tinted lens of prejudice, scrutinized as potential criminals. If only we could be free of all that.

Now and then when I am alone in the house, I lose myself in these idle fancies, and at some point I began to reveal them to the local Party secretary. While others have shunned or spied on us, he has been making a point of dropping by to see how I am. His advice is fair and open-minded, encouraging me to support my husband in whatever way I can. I am eternally grateful to him.

13th November

As I felt around at the back of the quilt cupboard, my heart lurched. The contraceptives I hid in the corner had vanished. A mouse? No, that wasn't possible. Min-hyuk, then? No, he wasn't the type to get up to such tricks. There was only one possible culprit—my husband. All I can do now is hope that he hasn't realized what they are. . . . But if he didn't suspect anything, surely he would have just asked me what they were? He's been too patient and too tactful to say anything, but I know he's been waiting for a pregnancy. What will he do now? What excuse can I make that might convince him?

At all costs, I mustn't cause him any more pain. He's been hurt enough already.

But I just can't think how to help it. This is terrible, terrible!

21st November

It seems all my secrets are being found out. Today, my husband finally discovered the meal I'd been making for myself—and he thought it was dog food! Dog food or pig swill, I should be grateful that it looked too unappetizing for him to suspect the truth. He's generally quite perceptive, but I suppose men are men, after all. I've been doing this for months—hovering around the breakfast table, finding something to keep myself occupied until he's practically finished eating, then sitting down for a few spoonfuls before seeing him off to work. The food that was meant for me gets saved for my husband's lunch, but I have to boil up some scraps for myself to stave off the hunger pangs. I'd had to repeat this performance toward the end of each month, when I haven't managed to make the rations last, and he hasn't noticed a thing. Dog food! He headed back out with the tape measure, and as soon as the door closed behind him I could no longer contain my laughter. But the warm tears that trickled from my eyes weren't quite tears of amusement. Nor were they tears of self-pity, of course, that I had to live off such meager fare. I was simply upset by my own powerlessness; that this small act was all I could do for my husband.

19th December

It came completely out of nowhere, completely! True, I'd had my doubts for a little while now, but I never would have guessed his real intentions. It wasn't long after my husband had gone out after lunch that I heard the front door open. By now, I'd grown used to the local secretary letting himself in like that, as though this was his own home—perhaps it was the frequency of his visits that made it seem fairly natural. But today I was taken aback to see him walk straight into the bedroom, before I'd even had time to come out and greet him. He reeked of alcohol. "Myung-ok!" he exclaimed, another startling thing—he almost always addressed me as "Min-hyuk's aunt." He slurred, "Have faith in me, and be patient," and sank clumsily to his knees. "Don't think that my efforts have been lacking. But for someone like your husband, joining the Party is no simple matter. Understand?"

Still on his knees, he shuffled toward me as he spoke, his breathing growing gradually heavier. The closer he came, the farther I shrank away from him, but now I found myself with my back to the wall. He should have noticed my discomfort and stayed where he was, but he kept on inching toward me, until his face was in front of my knees. "But don't worry," he said. "Everything is in my hands. In my hands."

He waved his right hand as if to demonstrate, then reached up and seized my wrist. My vision grew dark. What if Min-hyuk hadn't shown up just then, calling for me from the corridor? It doesn't bear thinking about. I dashed out to the front door and fumbled it open, with the secretary right behind me. He pressed himself up behind the open door, then slipped out when Min-hyuk wasn't looking.

I bit my lip, struggling to keep my composure, but was unable to hold back the tears. "Why are you crying, Auntie?"

32

Min-hyuk asked, clearly shaken to see me in such a state. I stammered something about having hurt myself. An excuse, but the pain I felt was genuine. To think that the faint glimmer of hope I'd been clinging to was in fact the dark shadow of wickedness!

Exhausted from crying, throat tight and temples pounding, I thought these feelings would never abate. There was nowhere I could go for help, no one who would right this wrong. The mere prospect of my husband finding out was enough to make me dizzy with fear. I felt mortified by that ugly scene, horrified at how I'd been deceived, and despairing over what might happen now. There was nothing else for it but to swallow it all inside myself, even if I choked on the bile. And just get through the days. Somehow . . .

Sangki!

Having dared to doubt such a wife, could I really call myself a human being? What kind of person, what kind of husband, would see only a mess of "dog food" and overlook the great love that lay behind it? Why hadn't I been struck down already, wretch that I was? What was the king of hell waiting for . . . ?

Not only had my wife suffered in silence, being snubbed and slighted for Min-hyuk's sake and subsisting on dog food for mine, but her sympathy for me had been so great that she'd even repressed that maternal instinct which craves a child of its own to love!

Sangki!

I closed the diary, faced with a reality I could not believe, could not bear to believe, yet finally, could not but believe. I sat hand in hand with my wife, we clasped each other tight, and I sobbed like a child. And then I made up my mind. We would escape from this land of deceit and falsehood, where even loyalty and diligence are not enough for life to flourish, choked as it is by tyranny and humiliation.

Outside the window, the cloak of darkness has already fallen. The clock on the wall shows that the hour is almost upon us. A few minutes from now, we will board a train that will carry us away from this town, all the way to the coast. There, a dugout canoe will be waiting, which I hid for just such an eventuality. My brother's family will join us, and the canoe will bear the fate of five lives.

There is, of course, great peril in this. We might easily be shot by the coast guard or a patrol boat, to be swallowed up like leaves in the wind and waves. And still, knowing this, we choose to bet our lives on this chance. Because we feel that to slide into oblivion would genuinely be better than continuing to live as we have been, persecuted and tormented. If fate intervenes, perhaps the hand of a rescuer might draw us to some new shore. Otherwise, we can only hope that our canoe on the vast blue will mark this land as a barren desert, a place where life withers and dies!

Il-cheol, who cannot say when he might see you again.
12th December, 1989

City of Specters

The day before the National Day celebrations, Pyongyang was decked out in all its finery. The past three months of tireless preparation had paid off in spectacular fashion.

When the subway train pulled into Pungnyeon station, Han Gyeong-hee only just managed to jump on, shoulder her way through to the back of the carriage, and grab the last available space. Underground, it was every bit as thronged with people as the streets on the surface. At each station, a tide of people surged into the carriage: soldiers, university students, middle-school pupils, young farmers hefting models for the ceremony, ordinary citizens bearing armfuls of flowers, Boy Scout leaders gripping cudgels. Their appearance, and particularly the things they were carrying, showed that they were on their way to the rehearsal for tomorrow's mass games, in which a million people would take part.

As more and more people piled on, Gyeong-hee was forced to wriggle her sturdy frame from side to side to keep herself from being mercilessly squeezed. Still, she kept her eyes on her son the whole time. The two-year-old boy was practically glued to her, sandwiched between her ample chest and her office bag. He seemed to cling ever closer to his mother, his wide eyes darting nervously around. The air in the carriage, a stifling fug of heat and noise that had worsened once the train pulled out of the station, seemed to cool off just a little, and Gyeong-hee could breathe a little more freely. As she did, she was able to hear again the voice of the nursery governess, ringing out clear above the babble of conversation and the train's clattering motion. In the nursery at the end of the working day, seeing each child safely into the arms of a parent, the governess had singled Gyeong-hee out for one of her lengthy spiels.

"Ah, Comrade Manager! I wonder, have you been scaring your son with stories of the Eobi, the fearsome creature who stuffs disobedient children into his sack and tosses them down a well? I ask because he was just having a nap earlier—your son, of course, not the Eobi, haha—when all of a sudden he jerked awake, covered in sweat and screaming as if he would burst. 'Eobi, Eobi!' Extraordinary to think someone like you could have produced such a delicate constitution."

"You're right—he must get it from his father's side. If he was anything like me it'd take more than a fairy tale to frighten him!"

Gyeong-hee forced a laugh. Though something of a celebrity when compared with the other mothers—manager of a marine products shop at the age of thirty-six, with a forceful personality that matched her strapping frame—she couldn't help being unsettled by the mention of Eobi. Of course, the governess had likely been speaking in innocence, mildly annoyed at having to deal with such a sensitive child and wondering how to prevent similar outbursts in the future. But Gyeong-hee wasn't the type to take such comments at face value. *Has the governess picked up on something?* she wondered. *Why else would she ask about the Eobi, of all things? How much does she know?* It was a futile train of thought, and she knew it. She berated herself for such spineless fretting.

And yet, after she'd got off at Seungri station and made her way back up to street level, the same thoughts began to crowd back in. Only when she arrived at Kim Il-sung Square, where an army drill was taking place, did a new realization come to her, one that trumped all her previous worries. Over the sea of heads and fists raised in salute, the window of her apartment was clearly visible, on the fifth floor of their building. All she had to do was cross the square to find herself at home. Today, though, this wasn't an option. Not because of the drill, but because entering the square would bring her son—already alarmed by the thousand-strong cries of "Long live Kim Il-sung! Long live North Korea!"—face-to-face with the terrifying Eobi.

"This kid!" Gyeong-hee muttered under her breath, barely aware that she was speaking. "A wet rag just like his dad . . ."

Abandoning her usual route home, Gyeong-hee turned instead to a nearby shop which specialized in children's clothes. Her son really was the spitting image of his father, with a body as feeble as his mind. What else but a congenital weakness could account for a child's throwing a fit at the sight of a mere picture! If it hadn't been for her husband, Gyeong-hee would have gone to the hospital days ago and demanded some kind of treatment. But no, it had to be kept hushed up. So the child was still a baby—what did that matter?

He was the son of a supervisor in the propaganda department, and having a tantrum at the sight of Marx's portrait had serious implications. And besides, now that the preparations for National Day were coming to a head, people were at such a level of excitement they'd be liable to mistake a dropped spoon for a grenade. The event itself would be followed by a strict review, and woe betide any participant who had demonstrated less than revolutionary fervor. No, it wouldn't do to step out of line just now. There were only a few days left, after all—they just needed to keep their heads down.

This was all Gyeong-hee's husband had to offer by way of a remedy.

The child she was carrying seemed to grow twice as heavy, and the sky, whose clear blue had been such a welcome contrast to the gray clouds of the past few days, began to stir with an unseasonal southerly wind. As they turned out of the alley where the clothes shop was situated, the contrast could not have been greater: from a lonely place where gusts of wind pursued fallen leaves and scraps of plastic lay idle in the gutter, to the vast expanse of the central road.

There, where the mass celebrations would soon be taking place, the street looked like some fierce wild beast, shaking its mane and roaring. Bristling with posters and placards, strong sharp lines of red writing that made the eye wince to look at them; lined on both sides with innumerable flags, their fabric snapping taut in the wind; pierced by shrill whistles, underlining each new announcement or command; rent down the middle by a dark blue broadcast car, blaring slogans through its loudspeaker, again and again so that the whole street rang with them. Punctuated every so often by a plane looming low in the city's skies, rising from takeoff or coming onto land; even their engines seemed to explode into an unprecedented roar, agitating the figures who moved below, causing them unconsciously to quicken their step.

As soon as Gyeong-hee arrived home, she spread her son's toys out over the floor.

"Look, my little Myeong-shik, don't these look fun? How about a little playtime? Beep-beep, ring-ring . . ."

Leaving him to his own devices, Gyeong-hee moved quickly to the windows and drew the curtains she'd put up. Their apartment was at the very front of the block, with one window facing south and another west. The south-facing window looked out onto the portrait of Karl Marx hung on the wall of the military department building, while the west-facing window framed a similar portrait of Kim Il-sung, hung near the VIP balcony of the Grand People's Study House. Gyeong-hee had to keep Myeong-shik from seeing those portraits.

But the white nylon under-curtain, provided as standard and kept drawn during the day, wasn't there to block the portraits out, and if anything the hazy shapes created by the curtain's thin gauze were even more frightening than the solid reality. Myeong-shik's initial terror had come from a face-to-face encounter with Marx's portrait, and with his stressed mind and active imagination, the picture loomed larger by the day.

It was getting on toward evening the previous Saturday when it had first happened. A citizens' rally was taking place in Kim Il-sung Square, with the aim of encouraging people to be ever more energetic in preparing for the celebrations. Everyone was pushed for time, so the rally had been organized at an hour when most workers would normally be heading home for the day. Myeong-shik had had a cold, and as Gyeong-hee, reluctant to leave him in that state, couldn't very well absent herself from the rally, in the end she'd strapped him to her back and gone into the square. Myeong-shik was prone to colds, seemingly a product of his weak constitution, but this was something different—his tiny body was burning hot against her back, telling Gyeong-hee that his fever wasn't to be dismissed as a mere sniffle.

Her group had been at the head of the square's far-left column, directly beneath the glowering gaze of Karl Marx. In the haze of dusk, before the square's electric lighting was switched on, that reddish-black face with its great swath of hair would have sent shivers down the spine of even the most stolid Party cadre. Perhaps it was that which accounted for

Gyeong-hee's unwonted recollection—a line from the first passage of *The Communist Manifesto*, which she'd read at some point during college.

"A specter is haunting Europe—the specter of Communism."

Had Marx inadvertently been writing his autobiography? The phrase was a mysteriously fitting description of how his portrait had appeared just then: closer in form to some spectral presence than an actual human being, plucked from some ghastly legend. Gyeong-hee's practical mind would never have normally entertained such speculations, but she was already anxious about Myeong-shik, worrying that he might somehow disturb the rally.

These fears had soon proved to be well founded; his nerves already set on edge by the mass of people around him, when the opening address boomed from the loudspeaker the boy was so startled that his vague snuffling transformed into harsh, desperate sobs. Gyeong-hee was sure she could hear people scolding her for bringing a bawling child to such an important rally, hissing at her to shut him up. She'd hastily swung him around to her front and rocked him gently in her arms, making soothing noises as loudly as she dared. But the boy just kept on crying.

Glancing around her, as a last resort she'd brought her face close to his. "Eobi! Eobi! The scary Eobi will get Myeong-shik if he's bad," she muttered. Still no luck. And then an idea struck her. This time, she held the boy up so that his gaze would fall directly on the portrait of Marx, muttering "Eobi!" in his ear all the while.

Myeong-shik had abruptly swallowed his sobs, and Gyeong-hee let out a sigh of relief. But the very next moment, the little lump of fire in her arms, who was pressing his face into her chest as though trying to tunnel inside her, became racked with the most extraordinary convulsions.

"Myeong-shik, Myeong-shik, no! This child . . ."

Gyeong-hee had been appalled. The corners of his mouth were flecked with foam, and his eyes were glassy and unfocused. Had a doctor happened to be at hand, the incident might well have ended in disaster. In the past week, Myeong-shik had had similar fits on two other occasions, terrified by the Eobi as seen through the apartment window. These convulsions could have been easily prevented if Gyeong-hee had been more scrupulous in her care—she'd drawn the double curtains only over the west-facing window, when she should have known to cover both. Myeong-shik was shaken from his senses by that initial terror; in his eyes the portrait of Kim Il-sung had worn the countenance of the menacing Eobi.

Now, though she had ensured that both sets of curtains were fully closed, Gyeong-hee was far from reassured as she watched her son find what little amusement he could in his toys. At any moment, she was expecting to hear the words "Fifth floor, apartment No. 3!" rapped out from the street below, in the chilling voice of the local Party secretary. If it happened, it would be the third time, and this time, she knew, he would not be fobbed off with an excuse and an apology.

"Fifth floor, apartment No. 3!"

Had she imagined it?

42

"Fifth floor No. 3!"

"Ah, yes." Even after she admitted to herself that the voice was real, it took Gyeong-hee a few moments before she was able to get the words out, and her casual tone sounded forced in her ears.

"Please come down."

So this is it. . . . Gyeong-hee lifted Myeong-shik up and carried him out of the apartment, descending the stairs with heavy feet.

"Again, Comrade Manager? After everything I've told you?"

Though well past forty, the local secretary's lips still bore the flush of youth, and her white-framed glasses contained no prescription. Her voice, on the other hand, was cold and colorless.

"The thing is, Comrade Secretary —"

"That's enough. Do I really have to spell it out for you a third time?" This appeared to be a rhetorical question, as the woman launched straight into her usual speech before Gyeong-hee had the chance to question its necessity. "Comrade Manager, do you have something against the white nylon undercurtain with which the Party has been good enough to provide you? Provided, indeed, as a special consideration for the houses in our street, which have the honor of being at the city's heart, a place where many foreigners will soon be visiting to see the celebrations. Do you perhaps resent the fact that they were not donated free of charge?"

"That's not it, it's just—"

"Look. Every other house has those same curtains, so the street can look neat and uniform. Which it would, if it your apartment wasn't sticking out like a sore thumb!"

Jabbing a rigid finger in the direction of the offending curtains, the secretary scowled first at them and then at Gyeong-hee herself.

"Well, as I said, it isn't that I——" Once again, Gyeong-hee found herself interrupted.

"It's the same story every time. Why do you persist with this obstinacy, Comrade Manager? You might throw your weight around in your job, but collective life is another matter!"

"You go too far. . . ."

"Too far?" the secretary thundered, though Gyeong-hee's protest had been couched in the mildest terms. She began to flip through the red notebook she'd had tucked under her arm.

"Given your family's loyalty to the Party, I'll tell you frankly how things stand. I received a report, dated the sixth of September. 'In apartment 3 on the fifth floor of Building 5, every day from around six in the evening until the next morning, blue double curtains are drawn in both windows. I find this extremely suspicious. It could be some kind of secret code, to communicate with spies.'" Clapping the notebook briskly shut, the secretary glanced sharply up at Gyeong-hee. "Such a report will have reached other ears than mine, Comrade Manager. And you dare to tell me that I'm the one who is going too far?"

44

Gyeong-hee's eyes were wide with shock—at first. Almost immediately, she felt something bubbling up inside her, moving through her body with real heat and substance. Those who have boldness—who are undaunted, even, in their endurance—know how to hold themselves in check when they have to. But there comes a point when that endurance reaches its limit, and when it does, the full force of their character will manifest with double intensity.

"'A secret code? Spies?'" Gyeong-hee's laughter finally burst forth, a hearty guffaw that she could not control. She laughed so long and so loud that Myeong-shik whimpered in alarm, and the secretary began to look somewhat cowed.

"Okay," Gyeong-hee said, still chuckling to herself, "I'll tell you." As she drew herself up to her full height, and shifted Myeong-shik higher in her arms, her imposing stature was matched once again by a dignified, commanding air. The laughter had acted as a coarse sieve, straining out her niggling concerns until all that was left was sheer brazen nerve. What could she possibly have to fear?

Even when she trotted off to school as a child, with her bowl cut and satchel, the red armband awarded to those whose character and comportment marked them out for a glittering career in the Party was a near-permanent fixture of her uniform, and it stayed on her arm through to her college days. After graduating and securing an enviable position, she steadily maintained her rank as a Party cadre and was entrusted with ever-greater responsibilities. Having a father who was martyred in the Korean War meant her standing was sufficiently secure to not be threatened by the minor slipups that were inevitable now and then.

Her husband, though the graduate of a distinguished revolutionary academy, lacked her confident, decisive outlook. Congenital timidity was the only reason to quail before the business of a child's nervous disposition! So their son found Marx's portrait frightening; did it follow that his parents opposed the man's ideology?

"After all," she continued, her voice made husky by a rumble of amusement, "can the full story be worse than what you think, that I should be denounced as a spy?" Beginning with the incident during the rally, Gyeong-hee rattled through the whole history of Myeong-shik's condition, ending with the business of the double curtains.

The secretary frowned.

"But why cover the window on this side, too? Marx's portrait isn't visible from there."

"No, but the Great Leader's is."

"So?"

"You know the saying: The child who fears turtles will flinch at a manhole cover."

"What? Your son is frightened by the portrait of our Great Leader?" The secretary's gaze seemed to sharpen suddenly behind her glasses, but Gyeong-hee was past being deterred by such things.

"In any case," she finished, "now that I've explained everything, I'd appreciate your understanding. I can't shut my child up in a cupboard, or watch him every minute of the day, so what else am I to do? But tomorrow, during the ceremony, I promise I'll keep the curtains open."

"That is not acceptable," the secretary insisted, her clipped tone rising as she delivered her final remarks. "This isn't some petty quarrel over home furnishings. The review due to take place after the ceremony is intended to weed out any deviance from Party ideology—you are aware of this, Comrade Manager? I've nothing more to say."

By the time Gyeong-hee had come up with a response, the secretary had vanished around the corner of the street, like a black hawk flying away with its prey.

Less than two hours later, both sets of double curtains were taken down in apartment No. 3 on the fifth floor of Building 5, though not by Gyeong-hee herself.

She was in the kitchen getting dinner ready, with a great banging of pots and pans and a slamming of cupboard doors, remembering the contempt that had laced the secretary's words. So when her husband entered the apartment, she didn't even realize it—he wasn't due home for another hour.

"Why have you drawn the double curtains?" Startled, Gyeong-hee looked up to find her husband standing there in the kitchen doorway, still clutching the handle of the door, as though reluctant to commit himself to entering. His eyebrows, two vivid black slashes that contrasted with his pallid complexion, curved up toward the middle of his forehead like the character for the number eight. "Well? Why have you drawn them again?"

Three vertical furrows appeared in Gyeong-hee's forehead as her hand paused in chopping the aubergine, producing the character for "stream" to match her husband's "eight."

"Answer me!"

Watching her husband dash over to both sets of windows and tear down the double curtains, Gyeong-hee left what she was doing and came out of the kitchen, picking up Myeong-shik from where he'd been playing on the floor.

The curtains dealt with, Gyeong-hee's husband turned back to her.

"I've told you time and time again to get rid of those damned curtains. As far as I can see, it just goes in one ear and out the other. If you were still a new bride fresh from the provinces then perhaps you'd have an excuse, but you've had more than enough time to get to know Pyongyang by now. How can you still not understand the way things work in this city?"

Suddenly deflated, he slumped down in his usual spot near the wall, still staring at Gyeong-hee in apparent disbelief.

"Wasn't I telling you only yesterday about the 'Rabbit with Three Burrows'? Like the rabbit who keeps three burrows to hurry into as needed, you can never be too careful. That's the moral of the story. Always stamp on a stone bridge before crossing, to check that it will bear your weight. Those are the rules for living in Pyongyang. So what on earth possessed you, today of all days?"

When no answer was forthcoming, Gyeong-hee's husband fished his cigarettes out of his pocket, stuck one between his lips, and lit it. He drew on it several times in quick succession, with a noisy smacking of his lips, released a lungful of smoke as a long sigh, and roused himself, somewhat revived.

"What's the most important theory in all of Marx's thought?" he asked, raising his arm to point to the man himself.

"Oh! First you talk about how long it's been since I was a new bride, and now you expect me to go back to the classroom?"

"The dictatorship of the proletariat. To which the theory of capital and the construction of scientific communism are both related, of course, but secondary. If capital is the weapon of capitalism, the weapon of socialism, which governs all our lives here, is the proletarian dictatorship. A dictatorship of the people! Yes, the people of this city understand all too well the reality of that idea. That's why they live according to the principles of the 'Rabbit with Three Burrows.' But you go about without a care in the world, thinking your martyred father puts you beyond reproach. What do you think that will be worth, the day you slip up and find the people against you? You think the Eobi is just a fairy tale?"

His eyes were burning with passion. When had her meek and mild husband ever shown such fervor before? But Gyeong-hee was too impatient to waste time wondering about this change.

"That's enough!" she snapped as soon as she had the chance. "I don't know what went wrong at work that's put you in this mood, but I haven't the time to stand here and be lectured at."

"For goodness' sake, how can you be so naïve?" Her husband stamped his foot in frustration. "'A bad day at work'? I've just come from the department of information!"

"The department of information?" Blanching, Gyeong-hee narrowed her eyes and studied her husband more closely. Then she laughed, relieved, as it all became plain. "Ah! I get it. Because of the 'secret code,' right?" She laughed again.

"What? You were called there too?"

"No, but our street secretary was just here, telling me all about this report that had been filed against us. She did hint that it might have gone higher up."

"And what did you tell her? About the reason for the curtains?"

"The truth, of course. You think that's worse than being accused of spying? A 'secret code'—ha!"

"There's nothing to laugh about, I tell you! I tried to explain that Myeong-shik must have inherited my feeble constitution, that that's why he has this condition, and do you know what the department chief said?"

"No, what?"

"That our physical constitution isn't all we inherit—that our mind-set comes from our parents too."

"He really said that?"

"Yes! And what would it say about you or me, if we'd passed on to our son a fear of the Great Leader's portrait? Well?"

"But that's ridiculous. . . ."

"Is it? It's as simple as two times two."

Outside the window, something glittered like the flash of a knife, followed by an almighty clang, as though a metal barrel were crashing down all five flights of their building's stairs. The wind slammed their front door shut, which Gyeong-hee's husband had left open in his haste; no sooner had the echo died away than it was replaced by the gentle drumming of rain against the windowpane.

The rain carried on late into the night, repeatedly dropping to a murmur only to return to a fresh crescendo. Myeong-shik's sleep was so fitful it barely warranted the name, and Gyeong-hee had to sit by him all through the night, soothing each bout of tears.

It was the night before National Day, a day of celebration which the entire city had been anticipating for months, and Gyeong-hee was so exhausted that she nodded off time after time as she sat by her son. Each time the rain slackened, the electric lanterns festooning the streets flickered back on again, their light causing multicolored flowers to bloom on the windowpanes. Had it been a different holiday, the Lunar New Year or Harvest Festival, the sight would have lightened Gyeong-hee's spirits, but these lights just seemed to mock her.

As she'd drop off, then startle herself awake again, her hand would automatically feel for Myeong-shik. But then her head would resume its jerky nodding, like a pestle pounding rice flour.

The surge of the rain, the sighing of the wind, the night lying otherwise silent in the streets—eventually, all these disjointed elements came together to formn a single dissonant chord, unfurling an alien cityscape in Gyeong-hee's exhausted mind. A drawn-out cry blew in from somewhere, reverberating throughout the sleeping city. *"Eo-bi"*

"What are you doing hanging around when you should be asleep at home? Planning to spoil tomorrow's celebrations?"

But what was this? A monstrous, hairy figure straddling two of the tallest apartment buildings, a foot on each roof? It was! None other than the Eobi himself!

So horrified that her wits deserted her, Gyeong-hee turned and ran for her life. But the tense little faces peering out of each window, as densely as the cells in a hive, scrutinizing the movements in the street below, belonged not to people but to rabbits! They were the rabbits from the fable, the one her husband had learned by heart as a child. But how had Gyeong-hee become trapped inside it?

Frantically scanning her surroundings—she was back in her apartment now, but the nightmare was ongoing—she spotted another of the rabbits lying stretched out on the bed over there, a particularly pathetic-looking specimen. Its mouth formed a pitiful O of surprise, but it was fast asleep and snoring thunderously. It must have been the Eobi's harrying roar that had left it so drained! But what was that row of small white teeth she glimpsed inside its gaping mouth? Why, it wasn't a rabbit at all—it was her husband!

"Ma-ma!"

"Oh, oh! Sleep, sleep, Myeong-shik. . . ."

Even in the grip of her trance, Gyeong-hee had been mechanically going through the motions of soothing the restless

Myeong-shik, but now her movements began to slacken again, little by little. She slipped into that same sleep in which, in spite of the howling wind, the exhausted city was readying itself.

As soon as the next day dawned, people rushed to their windows to peer anxiously upward. Young or old, man or woman, there couldn't have been a single person in the whole city who wasn't examining the sky, trying to second-guess the weather. The signs were far from promising—the sky was covering itself with ink-black clouds, threatening an escalation in the already steady rain.

Around six o'clock in the morning, though, it appeared that this was a false alarm—the rain petered out, and the sky showed its face as though nothing had ever happened. In the barracks, schools, and factories, the hundred thousand ceremony participants began to stir themselves, all according to plan.

But not even thirty minutes had gone by before the sky put on another bombastic display. This time the rain went well beyond a mere shower, pouring down in great, vigorous sheets, enough to throw the whole city into turmoil. Sewers overflowed into seething gutters, and people sought refuge anywhere they could—in subways and apartment buildings, in underground stations and bus stop shelters, beneath the awnings of public buildings or the lintels of front doors—watching the raging torrent with dismay.

Eight o'clock went by, then nine o'clock. . . . Only when the clock hand showed a scant forty-five minutes remaining before the ceremony's scheduled start time of ten o'clock did the rain abruptly cease, as though the sky were giving its reluctant permission for everything to go ahead as planned. A rainbow strung itself between Yanggak Isle and Moran Peak, like a banner that might have read "Impossible to Hold Ceremony at Scheduled Time." Patches of clear blue began to show through, and all the signs pointed to a day of glorious sunshine.

Now the ceremony would be able to go ahead as planned, with the cleanly washed city as a stylish backdrop—if the hundred thousand people scattered throughout the city center could manage to converge on Kim Il-sung Square within the next forty-five minutes. But that would have been like expecting new leaves to sprout from withered trees. In place of the rain, the sky began to crackle with innumerable radio broadcasts, including transmissions from the chief broadcasting offices of certain Western countries. "North Korean National Day celebrations, three months in the planning, postponed due to torrential rain!" Thus the foreigners displayed their ignorance of Pyongyang.

"Citizens, your attention. The ceremony will proceed as planned. All participants must, without exception, present themselves at their designated assembly point."

This broadcast on radio channel 3 shrilled its message into the city's collective eardrum. From the subways and apartment buildings, underground stations and bus stop shelters, beneath the awnings of public buildings or the lintels of front doors, people dashed out like bullets fired from a gun. Only

Gyeong-hee remained where she was, alone but for Myeong-shik in her hushed apartment. She heard the broadcast along with everybody else, understood the emphasis implicit in the words "without exception," but she knew she was exempt from her unit's roll call—she had a sick child to take care of. At least her apartment's enviable location meant she'd have a prime view of the ceremony. Moving to the window, she looked out over the vast expanse of the square—still deserted, despite the repeated broadcasts, and with only thirty-five minutes left on the clock.

Thirty minutes, twenty-five . . .

And then a miracle began to unfold. One by one, columns began to form in the square, neatly divided like blocks of tofu. Each column accumulated new blocks in rapid succession, as though the phrase "without exception" were a long steel spit pushing through the city, skewering people in bunches and delivering them promptly to the square. Eventually, with only five minutes to go, the entire square was a sea of color, with columns stretching out on both sides of Department Store 1, passing in front of the Children's Palace, and continuing all the way to the Yangcheon crossroads.

Senior state functionaries began to make their way out onto the VIP platform. A hushed silence descended on the square, which quivered with palpitations like the sea after a storm has just subsided.

"Informing the citizens. We have created a miracle here today, which has made the people of the world shudder with awe. One hundred thousand citizens have assembled here in

Kim Il-sung Square. One hundred thousand citizens within forty-five minutes . . ."

Unbeknownst to herself, Gyeong-hee pressed her hands together in front of her chest at this new broadcast from radio channel 3. For some reason, her heart began to shudder.

"Shudder"! Yes, that was the exact word for it. What had just taken place in front of Gyeong-hee's eyes was a spectacle inducing the awe of terror rather than the wonder felt in witnessing a miracle. Not even the threat of immediate death could have induced such unconditional obedience. What terrifying force had caused this city to give birth to such an incomprehensible upheaval?

As it turned out, Gyeong-hee did not have to wait long for an answer.

The postceremony review went on for a week in various cities throughout the country. At each unit's review hall, the Party secretary's sharp tone was punctuated by a strike of the hand on the rostrum. Those on the receiving end of this tongue-lashing would stand with their heads bowed, pressing their lips together to swallow stinging tears and stifle their cries of despair.

Anything deemed to have marred the celebrations, even down to a so-called lack of fervor, was exhaustively accounted for. The most severe punishment tended to be expulsion from the capital—"banishment" was the official term. This was effected with ruthless efficiency. The banished were not even permitted to pack their own belongings. Once the verdict had been handed down—"Comrade, your behavior at the time of the celebrations has been judged as unacceptable; according to Party regulations, your household will be relocated to the countryside"—the punishment was discharged immediately.

Under the careful scrutiny of a representative from the department of information, several officials arrived with straw bags and knotted rice sacks, into which belongings were packed so swiftly that the offenders never had time to react. Things were arranged so as to leave as little time as possible before the train bound for their new home departed. The representative stayed by the offenders' side the whole time, in the truck to the station and then onto the train, so deeply concerned to see them to their destination—which was so far from Pyongyang in every sense that it seemed an alien land—that he never once let them out of his sight.

All of which was exactly what happened to Gyeong-hee and her family. The verdict was just as her husband had predicted: "Neglecting to educate their son in the proper revolutionary principles, with a negative effect on the National Day ceremony; further, making coarse remarks about the portrait of Karl Marx, the father of communism, and comparing the portrait of our Great Leader to a manhole cover. The accused are therefore guilty of jeopardizing the preservation of our Party's ideology. . . ."

There were four passengers in the truck, which left close to midnight, the icy chill of mid-September biting down to the bone: Han Gyeong-hee, her husband Park Sung-il and son Park Myeong-shik, plus the representative from the department of information, crouching in the cargo space among the family's belongings. The seat next to the driver was free, but the representative, ever solicitous of his charges, had elected to stay next to the family.

The baby cried and cried. His exhausted, monotonous sobs, and the hemp hood that had been tied under Gyeong-hee's chin, created a vivid picture of the family's suffering. Her husband chain-smoked throughout the journey, and when a spark from his pipe landed on one of the bundles of clothes, burning a small hole through the fabric, no one moved to brush it off.

Before he left, the driver had to bend over the engine, coaxing the sputtering machine into life. Even that brief space of time was enough for a multitude of thoughts to come piling into Gyeong-hee's mind. They popped up one after another, a bewildering procession of disjointed fragments. There were the potsherds she'd used to serve up a meal of sand, when she was still young enough to play at keeping house, and the time she'd scrapped with the neighbor's son, who'd dared to call her a tomboy. Or that winter vacation in her first year of college, when she arrived home after taking the night train alone across the country, a distance of some thirty *ri*. "Look at this girl!" her grandmother had exclaimed. "Does she know no fear? She must be possessed by the spirit of some general!" And it was true—with a martyred father to give strength to her own inherent daring, up until now Gyeong-hee truly had lived in ignorance of what it was to fear.

Yet now fear seemed to govern her entire existence.

The door to the driver's cab banged shut and the engine roared into life. The sound scattered Gyeong-hee's thoughts, and her field of vision narrowed to take in only the window to her side, brightly lit as though someone were seeing them off. Gyeong-hee shifted and coughed as the vehicle jerked forward, trying to dislodge the column of water vapor that seemed to burn behind her breastbone.

Was it the knife-sharp glance of the representative that made her feel that burning sensation inside her? Or the decorative lanterns strung from the roof of the state department building, which seemed to command her to marshal her thoughts along the proper channel? Her blank gaze shifted, and the square's two portraits loomed into view: Karl Marx, his features buried in a bristling sea of beard; and Kim Il-sung, his lips set in a stern, disapproving line. Two red "specters" bellowing at Gyeong-hee: "Stop this useless brooding, Comrade! You dare to think your punishment unjust? When you're given an order you follow it, without exception. Without exception, do you hear? Don't you know to whom this city belongs?"

Those menacing, pitiless specters kept Gyeong-hee's grief inside her and crushed any hope of a reprieve.

Her limbs began to tremble, and not only because of the September chill. Fear swelled inside her—fear, something which had to be instilled in you from birth if you were to survive life in this country. Now, at last, she had the answer to the riddle, understood the force that had moved a hundred thousand people like puppets on a string. If her husband were to quiz her now on Marx's most significant theory, how much more seriously, rigorously, confidently she could have answered.

The truck raced on to the station. On both sides of the road, the clusters of apartment windows mysteriously recalled to her her dream from the night before National Day: the "Rabbit with Three Burrows". . . . Though it was close to midnight, Gyeong-hee sensed hundreds of figures hovering at those windows, peering out like rabbits from their burrows, eyes narrowed in accusation. If the Eobi were to give the order, the figures said, they would flock to the square in even less time than before, without exception!

April 1993

Life of a Swift Steed

A cold morning. The hard glint of snow lay over the land-scape, while the sky was threaded with billows of smoke, shivering up from the chimneys in brisk puffs.

Fumbling in his haste, Jeon Yeong-il unlocked the door to the office and rushed inside, straight over to the radiator, where he held out his shaking hands as though in supplication. The telephone was shrieking, but he could deal with that after he'd got himself warm. If that was even possible—he'd known corpses to give off more heat than this radiator. The boiler, intended for coal, was now having to run on whatever mix of damp sawdust could be scraped together, clanking and juddering as it strained to fulfill its function. Supplies of coal and firewood had also been cut off for the workers' hous-ing, meaning the factory's sole sawdust conveyor was having to feed their fireplaces too, fireplaces that had once seemed heaven-sent, a privilege reserved for those lucky enough to

61

have secured a position at the factory. Now, with the situation growing graver by the day, it was a job which pained you to the marrow of your bones.

"Damn it!" Yeong-il muttered to himself, feeling sorely put out. On top of the phone's incessant demands, his hands were stubbornly refusing to thaw; if anything, he was giving off more heat than that damned radiator, his own breath darkening the frost on the window which it had failed to shift. They were getting near to the point when the office would be thankful for the warmth of its workers, as opposed to the other way around. And if the supervisor's office, reserved for those factory employees with a star on their shoulder and a gun at their belt, had been reduced to this sorry state, what on earth were the rank and file having to cope with?

"Ah, damn it!" Cursing again at the obstinate telephone, Yeong-il snatched up the receiver.

"Hello, is this the factory supervisors' office?" a man's stentorian voice blasted out of the handset when it was still only halfway to Yeong-il's ear.

The man's severe speech impediment made him instantly recognizable: Chae Gwang, the military police's chief of communications. Not a man to be kept waiting; and yet, Yeong-il was too damned cold to be bothered with producing a response. Hopefully he could just keep mum, and Chae would get on with whatever he had to say.

"Hello! This is Choi Gwang!"

"Ah, hello, Comrade Chief!" Yeong-il forced a note of eagerness into his lackluster voice. "To what do we owe—"

"It's not as communications chief that I'm calling you today. This is a surveillance matter."

"Surveillance? Has there been some kind of incident?"

"Now, what was it . . . Ah yes! 'Irya Madya'! You've a man by that name in your factory, correct?"

"Yes, that's right, though it's a nickname, of course. His real name is Seol Yong-su."

"Seol Yong-su?"

"You never heard of him? He's a wrestler, or at least he used to be, back in his army days. He was quite a famous character, a regular strongman. . . . There wasn't a match that didn't end with him swinging his opponent up onto his shoulders, bellowing 'Irya Madya' like some kind of war cry, telling his horse to move faster. Though of course, he's got a fair few winters under his belt since then." Unwittingly drawn into the conversation, Yeong-il gradually forgot his numbed hands while explaining the history of this man Yong-su, which he knew very well.

"So that's where this bizarre nickname comes from, is it?"

"Well, not exactly. He's a driver, you see, has been all his life, and it's the phrase he uses to urge on his horses. He always sits in silence at our factory meetings, then the one time he decides he's got something to say he gets tongue-tied and starts mumbling nonsense to himself: 'Come on now, what was it? Irya Madya!' You know, as if to spur himself on . . ."

"Hahaha!" Chae Gwang's gurgling laughter sounded so absurd that Yeong-il couldn't help chuckling in response.

"It's understandable, though. He was as strong as an ox even as a child, but he never darkened the door of a school. It's quite a sight, him standing up on top of his cart, a mountain of luggage bouncing behind him, driving like the wind and shouting 'Irya Madya.' People in the street just stop in their tracks and stare like their eyes will pop out."

"Yes, yes, but what kind of man is he at his core?"

"At his core?" Yeong-il was silent for a time, beginning to suspect that this conversation wouldn't prove so easy to get out of. With his free hand he pulled the chair over toward him, pushed it right up against the radiator, and sat down. With the receiver clamped between his jaw and shoulder, he was able to hold both hands to the radiator. The telephone's kinked cord stretched taut, and Yeong-il himself was no less tense, as this already irritating conversation seemed to be taking a sinister turn, with Chae Gwang angling for information on Seol Yong-su.

The deep bond between Yeong-il and Yong-su was an open secret within the factory walls. There was almost no one who didn't know that Yeong-il's father and Yong-su had grown as close as brothers during the years of the Japanese occupation, their friendship cemented by shared hardships and a series of close shaves with death. Through the decades following liberation that friendship never wavered, and a few years ago, when Yeong-il's father died, the close relationship had been passed to his son, who still referred to Yong-su affectionately as "Uncle." Now that Chae Gwang, of all people,

64

was grubbing around for information, Yeong-il couldn't help feeling uneasy.

Chae Gwang assumed that the long silence was due to Yeong-il's rummaging around for Yong-su's official documents, and his patience was reaching its limit. He loudly cleared his throat.

"I have it, Comrade Chief. . . . At his core, he's someone whose work has never given cause for complaint." Yeong-il said this firmly, as though drawing a line under the matter. But Chae Gwang wasn't to be put off.

"That's not saying much," he snapped. "Don't beat around the bush, man. I want specifics."

"Very well. He joined the Communist Party immediately after liberation and was decorated for his heroism during the war. A revolutionary worker, in other words, who has dedicated himself solely to the establishment and preservation of socialism, alongside his work as a coach driver. In fact, I've just come from a medal-giving ceremony, and once again it was Seol Yong-su's name called. Second Order of Merit. He must have a dozen awards by now."

"And why do you think that is?" Now was the time to risk the question which Yeong-il had been itching to get off his chest. There might not be a better opportunity.

"What's happened, exactly, Comrade Chief?"

"There's an old tree in this man's yard, am I right?"

"Yes, that's right, a large elm."

"And the military police telephone line passes very close to that elm."

"Yes, and so?"

"And so, our men went to disentangle the line the day before yesterday, and as the tree was in their way, they decided to cut one of its branches off—a single branch, you understand."

"And?"

"And do you know how this 'Irya Madya' reacted? He went completely berserk, like he was having some kind of fit, rampaging around and threatening to take his axe to whoever dared even touch his tree. Waving an actual axe in their face!"

"An axe?"

"An axe! Meaning my men came back without having done their job. Imbeciles. They've been severely reprimanded, of course. I won't have some old man defying me!"

This last exclamation was accompanied by a terrific thud, presumably the sound of Chae Gwang thumping his desk. Yeong-il could almost see him—red in the face and round as a jar, fairly quivering with apoplexy—and the image was so ridiculous that a trickle of laughter broke through the tension. That pigheaded man would make a mountain out of a molehill, given half the chance—something it occurred now to Yeong-il that he ought to prevent.

"Haha, Comrade Chief! You know, it doesn't do for someone of your magnificent girth to agitate himself."

"What?"

"What I mean is, getting worked up over such a trifling matter is liable to harm your health. There's a story behind that elm, you see, which might explain Seol Yong-su's reaction."

"Story? You think I have time for stories?"

"You see, old Yong-su planted that tree himself back in 1948, to commemorate his joining the Party."

"Oh, so it's a 'special' tree is it?" Chae Gwang sneered. "I'm shaking in my boots!"

"That's right, a very special tree." Yeong-il had to struggle to maintain an even tone, and to swallow the words which had rushed up unbidden to the tip of his tongue: that there was also an elm in the yard of his own house, the house he had inherited from his father, an elm that had been planted on the same day and for the same reason.

Once the Japanese army had been defeated and the Korean Peninsula liberated, the ideals of the newly established Communist Party had been music to the ears of the two sworn brothers, who had both spent the occupation years toiling at a labor camp, driving teams of horses and cattle to haul logs for construction. They joined the Party together, on the same hour of the same day, their heads filled with dreams of prosperity.

Yeong-il was still a shaven-headed lad when he'd first learned the true significance of the tree. He'd been pestering his parents for a new tracksuit—Labor Day must have been coming up—and eventually his father had become so sick of his whining that he'd given him a sharp clip around the ear. Bawling at this bad treatment, Yeong-il had immediately gone in search of his "uncle." He found him in the stable, giving the walls a fresh coat of plaster before winter set in and the horses would have to be brought inside. Standing on the dirt floor in his bare feet, the older man turned and gave the boy a friendly greeting, then stood there in silence, hands on hips, as Yeong-il blurted out the story of his woes.

"What, some big hairy grown-up hit our Yeong-il? Where is he, eh? You just take me to him, then we'll see what's what!" Setting down his plastering trowel, Yong-su beckoned the boy over and sat him on his knee, wiping away the tears and snot that were streaming down his face. "Yeong-il!" he said, continuing in a conspiratorial tone: "Your house has got a tree just like that one, right?" Yeong-il's gaze followed his uncle's finger to the sapling visible through the stable door, but he was still too upset to do more than nod in answer. "Well, do you know what kind of tree it is?"

Put out by what he considered a blockheaded question, Yeong-il recovered his voice. "An elm, of course."

"Yes, but it's not just any old elm—it's a magic elm."

"A magic elm?"

"That's right! When it grows to be as tall as that chimney over there, sugar candy and honey cookies will rain down from it, thick as leaves."

"Pfft, that's a big fat lie."

"It's all true! When has your uncle ever lied to you?"

"But what about my tracksuit?"

"A tracksuit's nothing special—not like pure white rice with meat every day, and silk clothes, and a house with a tiled roof!"

"We're going to have all that? Wow!" Yeong-il clapped excitedly.

"But listen, Yeong-il! It's because we know that day will come that we have to really knuckle down now, and work as hard as we can to prepare for it. I have to work hard with my cart, and you with your alphabet—because we're establishing a new, democratic North Korea."

"But if we do that then it really will happen? Meat every day?"

"It'll happen for sure."

"Then promise!" Yeong-il stuck his little finger out, and Yong-su hooked his own calloused digit around it.

"It's—a—pro—mise!"

Even today, those chanted syllables reverberated loud and clear in Yeong-il's mind, suffused with the zeal of conviction. Of course, the story Yong-su told him that day wasn't something he'd concocted himself. The two men had heard these words at their district's Communist Party office, recently established by a cadre dispatched from Pyongyang, the day they'd shown up to ask for membership, shivering in the thin jackets which were the warmest clothes they owned. The story of the "magic elm" had been an additional embellishment for the naïve dream Yong-su already held, perfectly encapsulating his expectations for the new day that was sure to dawn. And that was the story of the "magic elm," its roots as deep as the living tree's, a story that summed up Yong-su's whole life.

But if Yeong-il was to make Chae Gwang understand the elm's full significance, he would have to relate the content of a certain article, which had been carried in the magazine

Chosun Literature when Yeong-il was still a boy. At the time, he'd read it so often as to have it practically memorized, and the intervening years had done nothing to dull the memory. Deciding that all he had to do was leave out his father's name, Yeong-il brought the receiver to his mouth again.

"Comrade Chief! I'd like to tell you a little more about this tree."

"Why not, when I've clearly got all day? Let's have it then, the dazzling exploits of this extraordinary tree. . . ."

"Well, there was an article once in *Chosun Literature*, with the title 'The Swift Steed Looks to the Future.' Here's how it went":

> For Seol Yong-su, the elm was a banner bearing the slogans of struggle, a placard encouraging him to keep up hope, reminding him of the blissful future which lay in wait. Even when the fires of war were raging, when he drove his wagon in a daring charge over a burning bridge, safely delivering its load of ammunition, and then during that difficult period just after the war, when he worked on the Haeju-Haseong railroad construction site, being eaten alive by lice and mosquitoes and living out of a grass tent, the branches of his elm fluttered like a flag in front of Yong-su's eyes, spurring him on to fresh feats of heroism with the promise of an abundant harvest, the golden fruit he would one day pluck from them. The deep bond between Yong-su and his elm was such that he even gave it the name 'Swift Steed,' the selfsame name borne by each of three horses

that have ever pulled his wagon. 'Irya Madya'! This is
the song that sums up his life, painting the picture of
communism's shining future, when everyone will eat
meat and white rice every day, wear silk clothes, and
live in a tile-roofed house.

"That's enough," Chae Gwang snapped in irritation, cutting Yeong-il off. "I've no taste for that puffed-up speechifying."

The condensation which Yeong-il's breath had formed on
the receiver, still sandwiched between his ear and shoulder,
was now forming thread-thin rivulets.

"And besides, if he really is as heroic as all that, all the
more reason for him not to hinder our work. Especially nowa-
days, when reactionaries around the world are slandering our
socialism. We cannot permit it! Who was that axe intended
for? . . . We must be stringent. No compromises, no exceptions. However red he might have been in the past, I can't
afford to overlook this current outrage. Not on any account.
And that's how it is."

Brusquely and without ceremony, Chae Gwang cut off
the call. And yet, Yeong-il didn't move to straighten up or put
the handset down at his end. In his mind, the thought was
slowly forming that it was he, Jeon Yeong-il, who couldn't
afford to overlook this business, though in a different sense
from what Chae Gwang had intended. Thinking, too, of his
deceased father, he felt certain that he had to prevent the fruits
of Yong-su's life's work from being pulled down around him.
And then there was another consideration: Were this incident

to leave even the faintest hint of a black mark hanging over Yong-su, suspicion would inevitably fall on Yeong-il too.

When Yeong-il left his house that night he had in his coat pocket a bottle of Kaoliang wine, which he'd asked his wife to get for him. Yong-su's home was only a stone's throw from his, so they would often drop in on each other, but today he'd felt unable to go empty-handed, conscious of the delicate matter he had to discuss.

As soon as dusk had fallen, the cold had shown a renewed vigor, and the pallid sliver of moon had retreated behind the patchy forest on the ridge of the northeast mountains, as though startled by the cracking of the river ice. Even with the collar of his coat turned up and the flaps of his winter cap tugged down, his forehead ached until it became numb and the flesh inside his nostrils stung.

But none of this served to deaden his thoughts. Whatever could have possessed Yong-su to behave so recklessly, and with military policemen to boot? As was often the case with physically strong men, Yong-su's simple kindness knew no bounds. He couldn't even force himself to apply the whip to any of his three "Swift Steeds." If such a man really had "waved an axe" in another's face, he must have had an extremely good reason.

Chae Gwang's knife was hanging over Yong-su's head, and it was up to Yeong-il to remove it; thinking this, he stepped into Yong-su's yard and came face-to-face with the elm that was at the heart of the matter. Though it stretched up almost as high as the house, it seemed to huddle there in the cold and the black, and the wind in its branches made a queer whistling sound. Sensing a human presence even through the stable wall, Swift Steed whinnied softly. Without knocking, as though he were entering his own home, Yeong-il pushed the door to the kitchen open. The shape and feel of its handle were almost as familiar to him as his own skin, though once it had seemed so much bigger in his palm.

Yong-su was sitting on the floor with his hands on his thighs, his back as upright as a stake planted in the ground, and when Yeong-il came in he turned his head but not his body, as though he'd been expecting the younger man.

"Where's Aunt?" Yeong-il asked in place of a proper greeting.

"Gone to the market. She got the train yesterday afternoon; we'd run out of everything, and she was hoping there might be some corn. I guess there wasn't, or she would have been back by now."

"So that's why it's so cold in here. Like an abandoned house."

"Come sit on this," Yong-su offered, smoothing out the worn old blanket on which he himself was installed. "This floor's like a block of ice."

It wasn't only the floor. A white layer of frost had actually formed on the far wall, around the hulking old-fashioned television and the chest used to store bedding during the day.

Yeong-il sat down where Yong-su had suggested, removing his hat but keeping his coat buttoned up. Only then

73

did he notice what Yong-su had spread out over his lap: a jacket weighed down with dazzling medals. Perhaps he'd been choosing a place to pin the latest addition, the one he'd received today, and had lost himself in reminiscence. But whatever old memories might have been revived, the freezing room and Yong-su's dark expression hinted that the joy they gave him was not unadulterated.

In any case, in an atmosphere like this, it was clear that Yeong-il would have to be all the more careful in broaching the matter at hand. Though normally gentle as a lamb, on one day out of a hundred, when something had roused him to behave rashly, Yong-su could be fierce as a lion, and liable to roar like one too.

Stumped as to how and where to begin, Yeong-il reached into his pocket and produced the bottle of strong sorghum wine.

"I thought this might help to ward off the cold. What do you say, Uncle, shall we warm ourselves up?"

"Ah, that's just the thing," Yong-su responded. "My throat was getting dry."

Yeong-il made to get up and go to the kitchen, but Yong-su laid a hand on his arm.

"Sit down, sit down. We've got everything here, don't put yourself out. . . ."

Remaining seated, the older man reached out and pulled over a small, low, rather shoddily made table that had been shoved up against the wall.

On the table were a soup dish empty but for chopsticks and a spoon, a small bowl containing some scraps of cabbage kimchi, the bowl's upturned lid, and an empty water glass.

"Well, go on," Yong-su urged, "pour it into one of these." Suppressing a shudder at the pitiful state his uncle's house had been reduced to, Yeong-il divided the alcohol between the water glass and the bowl lid.

"There," his uncle said. "Drink up!"

The harsh, raw alcohol made Yeong-il catch his breath almost as soon as he brought the lid to his lips, but Yong-su downed his in a single gulp, as though it were nothing stronger than beer. It wasn't usually his way, but today it was as though a stiffness had come over him, which was able to relax only after a strong drink. Once he'd emptied two cups in rapid succession, he began to roll himself a cigarette. This proved to be rather a lengthy process, what with his eyes and his hands constantly straying back to his medals. Yeong-il was finding himself similarly enthralled, though he couldn't have said why. After all, they were as familiar to him as if they'd been his own; he could reel off the story behind each one almost without thinking. How many times had he done just that, as a ruddy-cheeked schoolboy boasting to his classmates about the great achievements of his uncle and his father!

Occupying pride of place at the top was the soldier's honor medal, received for having driven his ammunitions wagon over a wooden bridge engulfed by flames; beneath that, the First Order of National Merit, for his work on the construction of the Haeju-Haseong railroad; beneath that, a Labor Medal and another Award of Merit, awarded, respectively, at the construction camp of the 2.8 Vinylon factory, a textile fiber launched in 1960, and the Seodusu power plant.

Reckoning it up by these medals, you could see that the main chunk of his life, around forty years out of fifty-six, had been spent either on the field of battle or at various construction sites. And it was precisely in those days of dust and lack that Yong-su had acquired his reputation as "Communism's Swift Steed," the revolutionary wagon driver whose brawny frame meant he even loaded his wagon himself rather than employ an assistant as the other drivers did. And yet, whatever the circumstances, he was always quickest to load and unload, swinging huge packs up onto his shoulders as easily as he lifted his opponents in the ring. All this meant his brow sparkled with sweat the whole year round, and the heels of his trainers would wear away within the space of ten days.

Such were Seol Yong-su's medals, salted with his own sweat and blood, tempered in wind and rain. Today another medal, perhaps the last, had been added to this hoard, so how could he be expected to keep his thoughts from drifting away on the waves of memory?

Yong-su noisily blew out a stream of smoke, and Yeong-il finally managed to tear his gaze from the medals.

"You must have a lot on your mind, Uncle? Receiving your thirteenth medal, I mean."

"That's right. Before you arrived, I was just thinking about the true owner of these medals."

"What are you talking about, true owner? They were each awarded to you for your unsparing devotion to this country!"

Yong-su was silent, visibly hesitating over whether or not to speak what was on his mind. After a while, he continued. "The true owner of these medals . . . is standing outside."

"What? Outside?" Yeong-il blanched. "You don't mean . . ."

"Why so startled? That's right, I'm talking about that elm tree out there. That's what's had me on my feet my whole life, working myself to the bone! Every time I looked at it, it's like I could see them come to life—all the promises they made me when I was a lad. All the wonderful things that were going to come true. It's that elm that's spurred me on to do the things they gave me these shiny medals for; and yet, in the end . . ."

"But this is exactly what my father said to me! The evening before he died, he gazed at the elm outside our window and said the same thing you've said to me. That was one thing, but hearing them again now . . ."

"Of course he did! That little brother of mine was another one who spent his life slaving away for the dazzling dream promised by that elm. He had ten medals all told, didn't he? For his pains."

"That's right. The tenth was his last."

"The tenth—ha!—and all thanks to that elm!" Yeong-il thought he spotted a way in, to broach the subject that their conversation had been circling around.

"So, Uncle, you're saying that you've been thinking a lot about that elm this evening?"

"Why wouldn't I have been? Ever since I first became a Party member, that elm has been my rock, a pillar propping me up. And isn't it also what's brought you here today?"

"Oh, no!" Yeong-il blustered, caught off guard by this turning of the tables. He'd only ever known his uncle as a simple soul; now it seemed he'd been hiding another man inside him, one who was shrewd and perceptive! In any case, it was lucky that Yong-su had been the one to mention the elm himself.

"All right, let's have it," Yong-su said, with an air of pulling down a veil. "You've come to ask me about that business the other day, haven't you? Those military police goons who tried to cut down my tree."

"I have," Yeong-il admitted with an apologetic smile, grateful for his uncle's understanding.

"Well, it's as I thought. Do these men ever quit?"

"But what happened exactly?" Reassured, Yeong-il felt able to cut right to the heart of the matter. "Is it true what I've been told, that you waved an axe at them?"

"True, well, yes . . . and then again maybe not. Lightning always strikes some innocent toads, or so they say."

"Toads? What . . . Uncle, now that we've got around to it, please let's stick to what's important. I need to hear your side of the story. . . ."

"Well, and why not? I've nothing to fear, after all. The fact is that right before it all kicked off—yesterday lunchtime, that is—me and your aunt had been having a fair old bust-up."

Yong-su fell silent, and Yeong-il began to roll himself a cigarette while he waited for his uncle to find the thread of his story. These days even the military police were having to tighten their belts, meaning Yeong-il too had been reduced to roll-ups.

"The reason we were arguing . . ." Yong-su went on. "Well, I'd just come home for lunch, and I knew I had to be quick, so I left my wagon outside, with Swift Steed still hitched up. I'd barely finished chewing when your aunt started clearing the table, bustling around telling me to get my quilted jacket on—she was already wearing hers. I was wondering what she had to do that was so urgent, when she noticed that I'd begun to roll myself a cigarette. And do you know what she said? 'The winter sun sets swifter than a pea rolling off a monk's head, and you want to smoke the day away?' Come here!"

As he sat there listening to his uncle's story, the smoke from Yeong-il's cigarette quietly unspooled into the freezing air, and a space gradually formed between the two men.

"What? What are you saying?" Yong-su regarded his wife with suspicious puzzlement, and her own gaze instantly hardened.

"So you're not going today either?" Only then did Yong-su recall the conversation they'd had the previous day. Damn it!

"I've already cut off the branches and stripped the bark," his wife had said, "so there's only the trunk left. But it's too

79

heavy for me to manage on my own. It's not far, only in the Jeoldang valley, so can you come and fetch it with your wagon?"

This had come after she had acknowledged her worries about not having enough firewood, something she'd hitherto been keeping to herself. Yong-su had been coming home from work with nothing more than damp sawdust for fuel—and even that had been hard to come by; there was barely enough to fire the stove, never mind stoke the underfloor heating. Even steaming a cob of corn presented a challenge. This was no exaggeration. Recently, the number of factory workers arriving late to work had been increasing exponentially, and all for the same reason: because it was taking so long to cook even a small breakfast. If it hadn't been for his wife, whose white hair had done nothing to slow her down, Yong-su too would have been swelling the ranks of those tardy arrivals.

Yong-su was well aware that she had been spending her days rummaging through ditches and the like in search of whatever might burn, though he hadn't realized she'd recently been having to wander as far afield as the Jeoldang valley. If it hadn't been for the situation at the factory, she never would have waited so long to ask for help, for she had more than enough to deal with just to keep the household going.

But Yong-su simply had no time. These days, every pair of hands the factory could muster was enslaved to the needs of the boiler. Sawdust was a pitiful substitute for coal, and the boiler raced through it like fire through dry tinder, constantly demanding to be fed again even when everything that could be used for transportation, even handcarts and packs on people's backs, was employed to carry fuel to it. The broadcast car, which used to come out only at the beginning or end of the daily shift, and when things were particularly busy, was now harrying the workers nonstop, loudspeakers bellowing that if the boiler were to stop running, the steam pipes would inevitably freeze and burst, and then the whole system would be destroyed. . . .

"It's not as though I've not been worrying too, but I've had that broadcast car at my back the whole time. Don't you know how serious things are at the factory? Let's wait for a better opportunity."

Yong-su had said this so earnestly, so pitifully, that his wife hadn't had the heart to insist. The next day, the broadcast car had been back and forth shouting about the boiler right through the usual lunch hour, which was why Yong-su had just been shoveling some corn porridge down as quickly as possible, with Swift Steed still hitched to the wagon. However, it seemed his wife had mistaken the cause of this haste, thinking that he was planning to use the rest of the lunch break to drive out to the Jeoldang valley.

"How can you ask me to do this now, when you can hear the broadcast car just as well as I can?" Yong-su took a last drag on his cigarette, which he'd already smoked down to the nub, and stubbed it out in the ashtray. He gave an apologetic glance at his wife, who was still watching him with narrowed eyes. "I said we'd wait for a better opportunity—I didn't promise I'd go today."

"You don't seem overly concerned," she said in a choked voice.

"Just think for a moment. Right now, with everyone panicking, afraid that the factory boiler might explode, how could I save face if I went to fetch wood for my own home? People look up to me and my wagon, you know. And my elm . . ."

"For God's sake, not that elm again! 'My elm' this, 'my elm' that, morning, noon, and night . . . Where are the so-called fruits of this elm, eh, that you've worn your life out on? Still on their way, are they? Soup with meat and pure white rice—"

"Stop flapping your tongue, woman. They're awarding medals at the factory tomorrow; I'll need to be able to hold my head up then, won't I?"

"Another medal! What good is a medal to us? Will a medal keep us warm? Will a medal fill our stomachs? It's just a useless chunk of iron; it's a far cry from silk clothes and a tile-roofed house."

"What? You bitch!" Yong-su thundered, snatching up the ashtray. It flew past his wife's face, almost grazing her cheek, then smashed against the wall of the kitchen, exploding into a spray of fragments.

"I couldn't understand what the hell had gotten into her, talking to me like that all of a sudden. I was furious, absolutely furious. The slightest thing would have tipped me over the edge. And just then, the military police showed up in their fancy uniforms." Yong-su paused, seemingly struggling to repress the pent-up emotions that were flooding back again. "My wife had run out into the yard after I'd thrown the ash-tray, and I heard the sound of her arguing with someone, so I went outside to see who it was. And what do you think I saw? The last thing I needed right then, I can tell you. My heart was already ready to burst, and now here was some more oil to pour on the flame: those goons trying to saw off one of my elm's branches, and pushing my wife away when she tried to stop them!

"Well, as they say: For those who are a bit slow in the head, every slur cuts twice as deep. The axe was leaning against the wall of the stables, and I had it my hand before I knew what I was doing. The policemen just stood and stared while I bellowed at them: 'Touch even a single twig on that tree and you'll feel my axe. You and the tree both!' I was that miserable. . . . The men all cleared out of there quick sharp; if they hadn't, I don't know what might have happened."

After this speech of such unprecedented length, Yong-su clamped his mouth tight shut. Then, as though needing a drop of water to splash on his burning heart, he downed the dregs of alcohol still lurking in his cup.

Through eyes screwed up against the smoke from his third cigarette, Yeong-il was studying Yong-su attentively. On the one hand, Yong-su's last remarks seemed a clear enough conclusion to his story. And yet, thanks perhaps to his line of work, Yeong-il could sense that Yong-su hadn't said all he might have, that the words he'd ended with had others hidden inside. From the moment he'd entered Yong-su's house, he'd felt as though he were engaged in some form of conversational hide-and-seek. As a supervisor, he was used to having people behave cagily toward him; he'd just never imagined Yong-su would be capable of such tricks.

Clearly he'd been wrong. But if he was to extricate Yong-su from Chae Gwang's clutches, he needed all the information on the table. Most important of all was to clarify just what lay between the lines of Yong-su's story.

First of all, there was Yong-su's claim that he couldn't understand how he'd ended up hurling an ashtray at his wife. Why not? Surely he ought to disclose that much at least? All he'd said was that he'd been unable to control his rage at her comparing his medals to mere scrap metal, instantly robbing his life of its meaning.

Next, there were those two curious phrases he'd uttered: "For those who are a bit slow in the head, every slur cuts twice as deep," and "you and the tree both!" "A bit slow in the head"—that was a euphemism if ever he'd heard one, but what was behind it? And why would Yong-su have threatened to harm his precious elm? It wasn't as though he'd needed to make a confession in the first place; Yeong-il certainly hadn't been expecting it.

Now he saw it plain. A combination of recent events had led the scales to fall from Yong-su's eyes, revealing the always postponed fruits of his labor—that pure white rice and tile-roofed house—to be nothing but an illusion, one that he hadn't had the wits to see. He'd felt rage and sorrow, yes, but also shame at having been so easily placated, shame at the pride he had taken in useless lumps of metal; and so he'd wanted to punish himself, by striking at that which was most dear to him. . . .

Yeong-il was genuinely stunned. He would never have dreamed that that simple phrase, "waving an axe," could have had its roots in such enormous turmoil. And yet, even this was not as shocking as his own thoughts on the matter. Now that he had seen right through to the core of this man Seol Yong-su, a man who clearly believed himself to have been duped by socialism, how could he, an officer with a star on his shoulder, be regarding him with such equanimity?

Because of their intimate relationship? It seemed it wasn't just that. If you looked into it closely, the truth of the matter was that, considering what Yong-su had bumped up against in his life, wasn't it perfectly natural that he would in fact be jealous of Yeong-il and hold him in reproach!

Once Yeong-il's thoughts had reached this point, the floodgates were opened, and his boundless sympathy for Yong-su brought an ache to his chest and a lump to his throat. Seol Yong-su! Was there any man more worthy of pity?

What suffering could compare with the disappointment and regret that Yong-su must have felt when he came to realize that the simple faith with which he'd once shouted "It's—a—pro—mise" was founded on an illusion? He'd had to bear that acute sense of loss alone, with no one but himself to blame or reproach, the torment compounded by the lack of any outlet for it, the impossibility of allowing any outward expression. From that perspective, the axe-waving had been, not a threat of violence toward either the military police or the tree itself, but a cry of self-denunciation, the sound of a human being torn apart by contradictions.

Chae Gwang! You too ought to know the suffering of this man, a kindhearted man who has been cruelly deceived! That day will have to come, before too long.

Yeong-il stubbed out his cigarette. Yong-su, sensing a shift in his attitude, did the same.

The cold would not let up. The air inside the house was almost as bitter as outside, perhaps a sign of the impending turning of the year. The cold leached through the blanket they were sitting on, numbing Yeong-il's flesh, and the cloud of his breath was beginning the resemble cigarette smoke. He stood up.

"Where are you going?"

"Now that I've seen how the situation stands, there are a few things I've got to do."

"Very well . . ."

"But what are you going to do about the cold?"

"Good question. I feel like I'm sitting in a refrigerator, not a house."

As Yong-su raised his fist to his nose, clumsily brushing away the moisture that had gathered there, it seemed as if he had aged ten years in a moment. In the window's upper corner, a spider's web swayed gently in the draft, and the desiccated corpse of its maker rustled.

"Try burning a bit of the horses' hay. Then you'll be able to get some rest."

"You're right. I'll give that a go."

Yeong-il never imagined that this would be the last time he heard his uncle's voice.

The next morning, Yeong-il received a phone call saying that Yong-su had had an accident, and ran straight over to his house. More than the stiff limbs and shuttered eyes of his uncle, who must have died the night before, alone in the empty house, what startled Yeong-il was the body of the elm, lying splayed out in the center of the yard, having been hacked in two near the base of its trunk. The repeated blows had been delivered with such force, such frenzy, that there were tiny white chips of wood speckling even the stable roof. Stepping through the side door into the crowded kitchen, Yeong-il saw a block of elm wood burning in the fireplace, making a sound like the snickering of false laughter.

The coroner diagnosed the cause of death as a heart attack.

29th December, 1993

So Near, Yet So Far

"**A**i!"

A single cry escaped from Jeongsuk as, startled by the sound of the door swinging open, she sprang to her feet. Her son's diaper, which she'd just removed, dropped from her limp fingers and hit the floor with a wet smack. There in the doorway, filling the frame, was the husband she hadn't seen in so long. But her cry was not one of delight. She was astonished, and appalled, at how drastically altered he was.

Sunken cheeks, soiled clothes, the backpack that had been worn to rags hanging limp from one shoulder . . . He'd always been skinny and slightly stooped, but he looked to have aged twenty years in as many days. Jeongsuk would have mistaken him for someone middle-aged if she hadn't known better. Could a person be so radically transformed in such a short space of time? What had become of the man who had made only brief visits to the family home in the last couple of years?

"Ah, why do you look so shocked?" As though these words had released her from some spell, Jeongsuk ran forward and threw her arms around her husband's chest.

"Yeong-min's father! You're alive, you're alive, oh, oh. . . ."

"All right, don't carry on so . . . you'll wake the child. Our son."

"Do you know how long I've been waiting? Do you?" Jeongsuk's fists flailed at her husband's chest.

"You shouldn't have worried yourself."

"And how did you expect me to manage that? You were out that door without so much as a goodbye, never mind a travel permit. Angry. And drunk. How could I not expect the worst?"

"What happened back then . . . I'm sorry. Truly sorry."

"Oh, but what am I thinking—your mother's illness! How is she?"

"My mother . . ."

"Yes? Has she . . . recovered? Or . . ."

"No, nothing like that. Or, I don't know, in fact. I never got to see her."

"What?"

"I never even got to set eyes on the house."

"But then where on earth have you been all this time?"

"Please! I need a glass of cold water first."

Jeongsuk's husband threw open his jacket with surprising force, the zip screeching in protest. It looked as if he was trying to swallow something, his dry throat convulsing painfully. Jeongsuk hastily poured him a glass of water, which he drained in a single gulp. Handing the empty glass back to her, he sank to the floor as though collapsing, and his gaze found its way to their son.

"Our Yeong-min's grown so much. . . ."

Jeongsuk frowned, alarmed by the note of dull fatigue in her husband's voice; he was like someone whose strength had been sapped by long illness. *He must be exhausted,* she thought. *And when would he last have eaten?*

"You stay and rest with Yeong-min, then," she said brightly. "I'll just go and see about something to eat." She hurried into the kitchen and started to wash some rice, then paused.

"Would you like to wash your face first?" she called out. "I can run you some water."

There was no answer. Peering around the kitchen door, Jeongsuk was shocked to find that her husband had fallen sound asleep. With his mouth hanging open in his pale, gaunt face, he looked more like a corpse than a living man. A louse emerged from his sweater and crawled downward over his trousers, its white body evident against the coarse black material. Jeongsuk darted forward to snatch it up and crush it, shuddering with disgust at what she was witnessing, and tears sprang again into her eyes. What had been done to her

91

husband, a kind, unassuming man, despite his imposing height, for him to return in such a state?

For the next three days he slept like the dead, clearly ill from exhaustion. Only by the fourth day had he recovered his strength enough to tell Jeongsuk the full story of what had happened to him.

His mother is dressed in white, standing on a hill that looks down on his home village, the blue river gleaming below. But she is ill—how has she been able to leave the house? The boatman plies his oars diligently, setting up a rhythmic creaking, but to Myeong-chol they seem to be moving in slow motion.

"Yeong-min's father!"

His mother runs right to the bank of the river, arms open to embrace her son, as though unwilling to delay the moment of their reunion even a second more. Equally impatient, Myeong-chol rushes forward before the boat has even bumped up against the jetty, but stumbles and pitches over the side, headfirst into the water. How deep it is, even this close to the shore. . . . And just as that thought pops into his head he sinks swiftly out of sight, down, down into the river's depths. Thrashing and flailing, he manages to get his head back above the surface, but sees, to his dismay, that the strong current has already forced him back toward the middle of the river!

"Myeong-chol!"

He can just about glimpse his mother running along the bank, her face now as white as her clothes.

"Mother! Mother!" he shouts back to her, and, with a strength born of desperation, windmills his arms to propel himself toward her.

A hand clasps Myeong-chol's shoulder and shakes him, firmly but gently.

"Y-yeah? . . . Yeah?"

As the dream dissolved, Myeong-chol opened his eyes. Who was this young man peering down at him, and why did he look so anxious? As his mind gradually sharpened, the sound of a train's wheels clattering over the track pulled into focus. Huddled in his seat in a corner of the carriage, Myeong-chol immediately sat up straight.

It had to be late at night indeed, as even those crammed into the train's passageway were lost in their dreams, their faces buried in their laps.

"You're finally awake!" The young man kept his voice down, but his relief was plainly audible. "Just take a moment. Think carefully before you do anything. You don't have a travel permit, or a ticket either. You were drunk, you see."

This news had the same effect on Myeong-chol as being doused with cold water. He was now perfectly alert and aware of his surroundings, and the course of events that had led to this predicament played in his mind as a moving panorama.

A smothered silence reigned in the waiting room of Department Two. This stifling atmosphere was due not only to the great number of people packing the tiny room, all of them waiting their turn, holding their breath, nor only to the oppressive heat of the midsummer sun beating down in the streets outside. It also came from all the notices of "Regulations of Travel," so numerous there was barely any wall left visible, and the shrill little phrases they bore: "'fine"; "forced labor"; "legal sanctions." And finally, it came from the pair of voices at the glass-fronted desk, which had a hole at the bottom like a ticket window, the voice behind the glass rapping out sharply, the one in front tremulous, imploring.

Whether a given person's application was approved or denied was a matter of the utmost importance to all present, meaning that aside from the exchange between applicant and issuer, the air hung as heavy as in a graveyard, undisturbed by even a single cough. Everyone was well aware that only around one in ten applications was successful, so every time someone backed away from the window clutching a tiny permit slip, bowing and smiling in gratitude, a soft sigh of disappointment ran through the room like a breeze rustling the leaves of a tree.

Myeong-chol had to wait for over forty minutes before it was his turn to stand in front of the window.

"Yes, Comrade?" the permit issuer demanded, ogling Myeong-chol with his bulging eyes. He was a middle-aged man with a narrow forehead and a wide jaw, his gray-splotched skin like that of a frog in autumn; and he was perched on a tall chair like a judge from the Koryo Dynasty, so that even the gangling Myeong-chol had to tilt his head back to look his interlocutor in the eye.

"What's your business?" he snapped, raising his voice as though irritated that his questioning look had been insufficient. Myeong-chol was tongue-tied in the face of this aggressive attitude. That was always the way with him—whenever he came up against something awkward or perplexing, the words he had to say would just slosh around in his chest. Perhaps because there was so much he could have said, it all piled up and stopped his mouth like a cork.

How much he wanted to say right now—that he had just had a telegram reading "MOTHER CRITICALLY ILL"; that this was the third such missive he'd received this past month; that each time he'd applied for a travel permit to his home village his application had been denied; that a similar decision today might mean he would never see his mother again, at least in this life! But, cowed by those bulging eyes, Myeong-chol was able to produce only a muttered "I, this," as he smoothed out the telegram he'd been clutching in his sweaty fist and carefully pushed it through the hole in the window.

"What's this?"

"It's a telegram."

"You think I don't know a telegram when I see one? But why have you brought this to me? Your company has a line manager to handle travel permits, no?"

"Yes, and I did apply to him first, but it was rejected. . . ."

"Oh? So you thought, what, that you'd come here and get a permit for an application that had already been rejected?"

"It's just that this is the third time . . ." Myeong-chol produced two more telegrams from his coat pocket, limp, well-handled specimens he'd clearly had for a while. "Please consider my situation. I'm her firstborn, and her only son. There's only my younger sister left in our village, and she lives with her husband's family. . . ."

"That's enough." The three telegrams were swept back out through the window in a gesture of dismissal. "We've had an order from above forbidding travel to this district. They're gearing up to hold a Class One event—you know what that means, don't you? That's right, the Dear Leader himself. Now why am I bandying classified information with a witless mine worker?"

"Even so, when the mother that gave birth to you—"

"Enough! If you want to haggle, go do it at the market. This is Department Two, not some street stall!" The man's bulging eyes looked in danger of escaping their sockets. A sigh of defeat escaped from deep inside Myeong-chol, as though something had been snuffed out. Department Two was situated in the economy committee building, but in reality it operated under the purview of the military police. Its employees were security officers in plainclothes—was there anyone who wasn't aware of that? So why did this man feel the need to parade his authority and bluster about his time being wasted?

Making sure to appear suitably deferential, Myeong-chol withdrew from the coveted spot by the window. In his mind's eye, he saw his mother as she must look now, lying on her sickbed with only his sister to attend to her needs. He saw his little sister, who should by rights now be at her husband's house, and who must be listening every hour for her brother's tread! His poor widowed mother, who had never known any other life than farmwork, wearing away her feeble bones to raise her children all on her own!

Originally, Myeong-chol had planned to return to his home village after he finished his military service. He would labor alongside his mother, he thought, hoping, in whatever small way he could, to make things easier for her in the few years before she became eligible for an old-age pension. And then, of course, there had been the young woman—she would wait for him; they had an understanding. Even after he was discharged, and his entire platoon packed off to the Geomdeok mines, he'd been unwilling to abandon this dream.

What hadn't he tried to get away from the mines and back to his mother's side! He'd scrimped and saved to put together a bribe for the local Party secretary, repaired the mine foreman's underfloor heating as a favor, pressured a friend who worked at the hospital to forge a letter claiming his mother was gravely ill. Still, society's rules remained as rigid and unbending as ever, refusing to give an inch where Myeong-chol, so it was claimed, might be inclined to take a mile. Eventually he'd had no choice but to send for his intended—this much, at least, being permitted—and leave his mother all alone.

Time passed, as time does; Myeong-chol became a father, and his mother finally became eligible for a pension. There was only the upcoming harvest to be got through, then Myeong-chol could arrange to have her come and live with him and his wife. She would finally see her son again, and the grandson she'd never met! With the culmination of all his hopes so tantalizingly near at hand, how could he have guessed that those hopes would all come crashing down?

As he stumbled out of Department Two, his legs barely able to hold him up, a wave of soundless sobs threatened to choke Myeong-chol. His eyes, which shone with the gentle innocence of a calf's, brimmed with bitter tears. Was Solmoe, the village he'd grown up in, some foreign city like Tokyo or Istanbul? How could his own village, in his own country, his own land, be so remote, so utterly unreachable? He would have gladly trekked there on his own two feet, if only someone would have given him permission. A thousand *ri* or ten thousand, it didn't matter to him; if only those Travel Regulations weren't blocking his path.

Myeong-chol longed to let himself sob out loud, to stamp the ground or shake his fist at the sky. But, depending on the circumstances, he knew that even crying could be construed as an act of rebellion, for which, in this country, there was only one outcome—a swift and ruthless death. And so it was the law of the land to smile even when you were racked with pain, to swallow down whatever burned your throat.

Feelings of frustration and helplessness, of having been unfairly treated, left Myeong-chol physically and mentally drained, so that all he could do was wander the streets, wherever his feet took him, with no clear destination in mind. Everything was hateful. The chirping of the cicadas, which should have cut through the stifling July heat, was nothing but an irritating whine; both the ground he trod and the air he breathed were wholly repugnant. As he walked, memories of similar days were dredged up, days that were all too frequent in a life which, after all, could not yet be called long.

Like the day when, after graduating from middle school, he'd been called up to serve in the people's army—a decision in which individuals had no say—and seen his dreams of going on to university snuffed out. Or the day he'd been forced to trudge along with his unit, their destination written on a sign held up by an officer at the front of the column, then pile into the back of a tarp-covered truck, longing for home so strongly that he felt a lump in his chest. On those days, too, Myeong-chol had felt the need to weep and rail against the world; then, like today, he could only choke on his own frustration.

"Hey, is that you, Myeong-chol? Myeong-chol!"

Myeong-chol, who had been staring at the ground as he trailed along the roundabout, raised his head to see a stocky man with curly hair running across the new road toward him. it was his friend Yeong-ho.

"Well, how did it go?" From the urgency in Yeong-ho's voice, you would have thought it was his own application he was inquiring about. The two men had bumped into each other earlier that day, when Myeong-chol was on his way to Department Two. Yeong-ho, who'd been to buy something to drink to celebrate his younger brother's long-awaited visit, had stopped Myeong-chol in the street, and hadn't let him get away until he'd poured out all his worries over the permit. "Come on, tell me, did you get the permit or not?"

Aware that the news would pain Yeong-ho almost as much as himself, and overcome by his friend's empathy, Myeong-chol couldn't bring himself to open his mouth. Though they weren't from the same village, they'd joined the army in the same cohort, their friendship cemented when both were discharged and, against their will, started work at the Geomdeok mines. Both had become fathers relatively recently, and their wives had also grown very close, so each couple could be found in the other's house almost as often as their own.

"I knew it," Yeong-ho broke out, embarking on a rapid-fire speech in the hope of staying Myeong-chol's tears. "I knew that's how it would turn out. I didn't say anything when I met you before, thought I might as well let you hope, you never know, but you're not the only one who's been back and forth to Department Two recently. My brother's travel permit was approved ages ago, but it just keeps getting delayed. There's always some fault to pick with it—there are two of them on the same permit, you see, so they're both supposed to present themselves together at the factory, only the other guy got sick. What was my brother supposed to do? He explained the situation till he was blue in the face, but nothing doing. He hoped they'd show a bit of understanding—ha! Those bastards are about as understanding as a block of wood."

"I didn't even get time to explain; if I had . . ." Myeong-chol's throat contracted painfully, preventing him from finishing the sentence.

"Damn it! Come on, Myeong-chol, let's get out of here!" Taking his friend firmly by the wrist, Yeong-ho waved the keg of alcohol in his face. "There's only one remedy for a day like this—you need to get drunk, immediately."

The two men went back to Yeong-ho's home, where Myeong-chol did exactly as his friend had suggested. To make matters worse, they drank practically the entire keg between the two of them, as Yeong-ho's brother Yeong-sam refused to take more than a glass, wary of missing the evening train. Myeong-chol had never before drunk himself into such a stupor.

Yeong-ho, equally intoxicated, had the bright idea of using one of the telegrams as a travel permit, as they were about the right size. "If some bastard wants to look at it, well, he'll have a mother like everyone else, won't he? What dog doesn't have a mother? Permit or no permit, just go!"

Drunk as he was, Myeong-chol couldn't even contemplate following this advice. Taking pity on Myeong-chol, Yeong-sam suggested a slightly more practical plan: His own travel permit for that evening specified two persons, and as the other guy was no longer able to make it, they could at least go to the station together and see if they might just chance it.

Myeong-chol could only shake his head.

"I can't," he slurred repeatedly. "I don't have it in me."

"Ah, for God's sake!" Yeong-ho flew into a passion, banging his chopsticks on the drinking table. "They must have trained you well in that village of yours, eh? Properly broken you in. In this society, I tell you, people are like sheep!"

"Are you any different?" Yeong-sam countered. "If you hadn't been 'broken in,' as you put it, would you have managed to live so long?"

"Ha! Isn't that the truth. . . . Gah, Myeong-chol! Let's have a song, come on."

The train's whistle piercing the starless sky
Stirs the insides of the unfortunate man

Perhaps because one of the songs had been about a skylark, when Myeong-chol eventually staggered home his footsteps stopped outside his door rather than carrying him straight in. A birdcage hung from the eaves of his roof, containing a pair of larks. The birds were native to Myeong-chol's village, and his wife's brother had made her a gift of them on one of her visits home, having heard how intense Myeong-chol's homesickness was.

Though he had buried the placenta of his own son here in this mining town, to Myeong-chol these larks were the long, golden grasses and impossibly blue skies of the village that would always be his home. In the mornings and evenings when they struck up their song, he could swear that he heard that distant stream, the familiar tones of his mother's voice. That evening, as he stood and stared at the birds, his heart swelled with a passion intensified by his drunkenness. He unhooked the cage and held it in his hands, but it wasn't the larks that his dazed eyes saw; instead, it was the face of his mother, hovering on the brink of death.

"Mother! You've got one foot in the next world, and your son still can't come to you. I can't come. Mother!"

The front door opened and his wife ran out, disturbed by the commotion. Seeing Myeong-chol reeling where he stood, she linked her arm in his and encouraged him to lean on her.

"Come in and lie down. It's not your fault you can't go and see your mother. Do you hear me? It's not your fault. This society is too much sometimes. To tear a person up like this!"

But Jeongsuk's tears only fanned the flames.

"That's right, it's not my fault, it's not my fault. . . . I'm in a cage, just like this bird. . . . Damn it!" Gnashing his teeth, Myeong-chol unlocked the cage and flung the door open wide. The larks chirped in unison, as though to thank him, then stretched their wings and flew out of the cage, clumsy at first after their long confinement.

"That's right!" Myeong-chol muttered. "Go, go. You must have a hometown somewhere, too, and a mother who gave birth to you. . . ." He stared after the larks as they diminished to black specks, then vanished entirely into the blue. A spasm passed over his face, and he threw the empty cage to the ground. Seeing them soar so free, so far, had roused a burning envy in him, and a courage he hadn't known he possessed. "They're going, and I'm going too. . . . Yes, that's right, I'm going too!"

He slipped his arm from his wife's and dashed into the house, making a beeline for his backpack, already packed just in case the decision at Department Two was favorable. As well as a change of clothes and sundry necessities, it contained a package of dried fruit which was said to be good for his mother's heart disease, and which his wife had gradually gathered together from mountain foraging all through the autumn.

"What are you doing?" Jeongsuk cried in alarm, but Myeong-chol shook off her restraining hand and charged straight out of the door.

After that, Myeong-chol's memory was blank. According to Yeong-sam, it was pure luck that he and Myeong-chol had ended up in the same carriage. As soon as the younger man had spotted him and hurriedly helped him to a seat, Myeong-chol's head had tipped back and he'd begun to snore. Claiming Myeong-chol as the second traveler listed on his permit, and apologizing profusely for the state for he was in, Yeong-sam had managed to see them through four inspections without their ruse being discovered.

Now, though, he frowned, and brought his mouth right up to Myeong-chol's ear.

"I have to get off at the next station. What will you do? From now on you'll be on your own. You'll need to go 'underground,' like a real guerrilla."

Myeong-chol nodded his understanding, but the prospect of going it alone struck fear into his heart. He could feel the net closing around him, and a shiver ran down his spine. He would be caught; he was sure of it. Yet he never suspected just how soon he would find himself in that net.

Around twenty minutes after Yeong-sam had alighted at his station and the train had got back on its way, the voice of the attendant shattered the sleep of those who had finally managed to drop off after the latest batch of passengers had thrown the carriage into a commotion. "Permit inspection for all passengers. Please have your permits ready." As Yeong-sam had it, this would be the fifth such inspection since they'd both boarded the train, but to Myeong-chol, hearing the words for the first time, it was like a gun was being pressed into the small of his back. Two railroad security officers had already entered the carriage, one at either end, their blue uniforms making them look like venomous snakes as they shone their flashlights up and down the car. Myeong-chol's heart was hammering so loudly he felt sure his fellow passengers would hear it. His chest and back were slick with cold sweat.

"Hey! Wake up! Move, you filthy rat." At the sound of people being dragged from their seats just a few rows away, Myeong-chol's vision went dark. His rational mind lost any interest in dignity or shame, and his body took over, seized by the instinct to avoid discovery in absolutely any way he could. He dropped to the floor and began to wriggle his way beneath the seats, between the other passengers' legs, like an eel burrowing into the mud.

A fetid stench, undetectable from higher up in the carriage, now sat in his nostrils, and a spider's web snagged on one of his eyebrows. He contorted himself like a snake, his knees practically touching his chin, and cursed his unusually tall frame, which was protesting this treatment. Though he kept bumping his nose against shoes and trainers, in actual fact he was grateful for this thicket of legs, which screened the way both in front and behind. That gratitude, however, was fleeting. His blood seethed again. *What crime have I committed? Am I a thief or a murderer, to have to degrade myself like this? In this country of mine, is it a crime just to go and visit your sick mother?* He had a sudden urge to stand up and bolt straight out of the carriage. But just then, the flashlight's beam scythed right in front of his face, and he curled up as tightly as possible, even screwing his eyes tight shut.

"Permit!" That single word was like an iron hammer clanging down on Myeong-chol's head. Holding his breath, he opened his eyes just a crack and found himself looking straight up at the security officer's belt, visible beneath the bottom of his jacket, as he held his flashlight close to the permit in his other hand. That belt loomed over Myeong-chol, threatening to transform into the taut rope with which to bind a criminal. His spine broke out in gooseflesh. The officer had two guns. Might he not then also be carrying that same rope which Myeong-chol had seen all those years ago, stained with blood as it had been back then? The incident had been seared into his mind, and came back to him now in all its vivid clarity in spite of his present peril.

It had happened one spring day when Myeong-chol was still a lad, in his fifth year at school. Those pupils whom the school had decided were displaying counterrevolutionary tendencies had been marched out to a farm, lined up in the threshing field, and ordered to sit down. There, a condemned criminal was bound to the trunk of a peach tree beneath the glorious profusion of its blossom.

As the prosecutor began to recite his argument, recounting how the man had smeared feces on supplies that were to be exported to the Soviet Union, the criminal began to squirm frantically. Though he appeared to be yelling something, attempting to wave his arms in some kind of protest, the fact that his limbs were pinioned to his sides and a rag had been stuffed into his mouth meant that all that could be discerned was his desperate writhing, which grew gradually more and more violent. All of a sudden, his movements appeared to become much freer, as though one of his bonds had snapped, and a helmeted officer ran over to the tree. Grabbing a looped rope from his belt and stretching it out in a swift, practiced motion, he used it to bind the struggling criminal even more tightly.

Not long afterward, deafening gunshots rang out in quick succession. The metallic scents of blood and gunpowder soaked through the crisp spring air. A truck rumbled into the field and backed up close to the peach tree. Two security officers used their hand knives to cut the ropes around the tree. But the helmeted officer used his bare hands to untie his rope, stuffing its surely blood-soaked length roughly into his pocket. This made Myeong-chol's limbs tremble even more than the gunshots had.

Afterward, the memory of that rope had haunted Myeong-chol's days, an inevitable image in his dreams on nights when he'd been unable to finish his homework, when he would feel himself pinioned to the bed as tightly as the criminal had been to the peach tree. This period in his life marked a change in Myeong-chol; he began to feel ever more cowed and docile, rushing to obey whatever task his teachers or Boy Scout leader might set him.

That rope, which had inculcated a rigid obsession with obedience in the mind of Myeong-chol when he was a young boy, sought him out again when he was a man, on the day he was discharged from the army and packed off to the Geomdeok mountains. That day, when an escort officer climbed up into the truck with them, tasked with ensuring that there would be no attempts at desertion, Myeong-chol had glimpsed that rope hanging from his belt, next to a gun holster. Now, as he crouched on the filthy train carriage floor, his fate hanging in the balance, the idea that he might have to encounter that horrifying object yet again seemed the most terrifying aspect of the entire situation. It was as though he were being given a hint of a power that bound him tightly in its grasp, never slackening no matter how he tried to shuck it off. . . .

Even once the two officers had left the carriage, pushing and shoving a small line of those whose permits had not been in order, Myeong-chol barely allowed himself to breathe. He might have lain there beneath the seats for the whole duration of the journey, safely past the moment of crisis but afflicted by a fresh sense of needing to "save face," had it not been for a stroke of luck—a blackout inside the train.

With the interior of the carriage now as black as the fields outside, Myeong-chol lost no time in crawling out from beneath the seats and slipping farther along the train, in the opposite direction from that of the security officers, still clutching his backpack, with its precious parcel of dried fruit, which his fingers had refused to relinquish even at the very peak of his terror.

Over the course of the night and the day which he spent on that train, Myeong-chol seemed to become a different person. The hollow cheeks and staring eyes looking back at him from the carriage window were like those of a person wasted by disease. Which was understandable, considering that he'd had to dodge two further inspections, one by hiding in the foul-smelling toilets and one by lowering himself outside the wagon, through the window set into the upper part of the door, then holding on for dear life as the train clattered over the tracks. Dirty and dangerous as these options were, they were infinitely preferable to the moans and wails of those who failed the inspections and were forced off the train at the next station.

But all that was done with now. Now, with the stop for his village coming next, Myeong-chol had his sights set firmly on home, and forgot his own troubles for the first time since Yeong-sam had shaken him awake. Glancing at the window, he fancied that he saw his mother's face there rather than his own, and his hand strayed to the backpack in his lap as he thought about how glad he would be to see her, even on her sickbed.

Just as the morning sun was pushing above the ridge of Mount Seokda, Myeong-chol got down from the train, concealing himself in a small stream of passengers, from which he slipped away as soon as the coast was clear, clambering over the station wall without being spotted. It niggled at his conscience to be sneaking into his own hometown like some common thief, but his lack of a permit meant there was no other option. As the streets of the town petered out he began the ascent to Maldeung Pass, and there, at the top, he was able to look down on the broad course of the Soyang River, its sinuous contours so achingly familiar. Once he was across the river, it would be only a mere ten *ri*, crossing a single plain and skirting a single mountain, before he found himself finally home once more, in his own village of Solmoe!

Myeong-chol's pace quickened as he imagined setting foot in his childhood home; in his mind, he could already hear the snick of the latch lifting. Though the sun was now high enough in the sky for the heat to have built in intensity, the cool breeze off the Soyang River cut through it even at this distance. Myeong-chol could have sworn he could already hear the lapping waves, the piping of the waterfowl. To someone from Solmoe, hemmed in by mountains on its three other sides, the river was almost a maternal presence, and the scene of many happy memories.

Myeong-chol had been six years old when he'd first crossed the river, on a visit to his grandparents' house for the autumn harvest festival. No sooner had he and his mother alighted from the ferryboat than Myeong-chol had started pestering her to let them cross it again. His mother did all she could to dissuade him, reminding him that they'd be coming back that way later, but Myeong-chol insisted that they get back in the boat at once. In the face of such a stubborn passion, there was nothing his poor mother could do other than hold out another fare to the ferryman.

"Hang on," the old man said, frowning, "didn't you just pay me?"

"Yes, but my son wants another ride on the boat, and if I don't let him have his way I'll never hear the end of it."

"You mean you want another round trip? Back the way you came, and then back here again?"

"Yes, that's right. I'm sorry, I know it can't be easy for you at your age, but . . ."

"I never thought I'd see the day—a kid telling his mother what to do! Never you mind about any fare, just hop in. You too, my lad!"

And so, they ended up taking another trip across the river, back and forth, Myeong-chol giggling in delight. As soon as this jaunt was over, though, his mother had to stoop to vomit on the riverbank. The ferryman shook his head, regarding her with deep sympathy.

"Even in your condition you still gave that kid of yours his wish. . . ."

Myeong-chol had never forgotten those words, or the sight of his heavily pregnant mother smiling weakly through her nausea, one hand on her bump. It was such a precious memory for him that whenever he dreamed of his mother, as he had done on the train, a riverbank or ferry crossing would be sure to make an appearance.

Wait just a little longer, Mother! Soon you'll be the one who thinks she's dreaming, when this son of yours pokes his head around the door!

A fresh burst of energy gave wings to Myeong-chol's feet, and he flew down the path which led to the bridge, a cloud of dust in his wake.

"Halt!" Jolted out of his reverie by this abrupt command, Myeong-chol belatedly realized how reckless he'd been to approach so openly, heedless of the toll bar and checkpoint. Still, those were really only for vehicles; surely they wouldn't bother themselves with a single man on foot?

"ID papers."

The man who stepped forward from the sentry post looked to be around Myeong-chol's age. He was smartly dressed, holding a rifle pressed up to his shoulder, with small, downward-slanting eyes that resembled those of a crow-tit. Myeong-chol was rooted to the spot. He stood there blinking dumbly for a moment, then hurriedly fished out his papers. The sentry's eyes narrowed even further as he scanned each page of the document.

"Travel permit."

"I . . . don't have one." Myeong-chol had entered the road to unavoidable checkmate.

"What?" Those crow-tit eyes glared at him. "You've traveled here from Hamgyeong Province without a permit? When our district is about to host a Class One event? Unbelievable!"

The sentry blew a shrill blast on the whistle that dangled from his wrist, and the door of the checkpoint hut was flung open.

"What is it?"

"This guy's come from Hamgyeong without a travel permit."

"Well well, how intrepid! Send this hero in to me."

Confused by the tone of admiration, Myeong-chol walked tamely over to the hut and ducked inside the door. As soon as he did so, he realized his mistake. The man who'd called him in was a security officer, with a dark blue T on his epaulet; he was sitting in the hut's only chair, a line of men and women with pale, strained faces in front of him. He seemed to have been busy instructing them in the error of their ways, and seized on Myeong-chol's arrival as a helpful example.

"Look here. Travel between one county and another is controlled as tightly as possible, yet this goblin came crawling through in broad daylight!"

He jabbed a finger at the unfortunate Myeong-chol.

"From where in Hamgyeong Province?"

"T County."

"What do you do there?"

"I'm a miner."

"Indeed! And how is T County supposed to obtain its production goals with men like you running off? This is the chaos we end up with!" Still waving his hand in Myeong-chol's direction, the officer turned back to his captive audience. "Now, do we or don't we have to control citizens' movements? I mean, travel permits aren't only useful for catching enemy spies. Understand? I'm asking you, grandma."

"Yes, of course, but there's only one bridge between Ha-dong County and our Sangdong County . . . and my grandson got ill, all of a sudden. Well, at first it was just a cold—"

"Quiet, that's enough."

If a truck hadn't pulled up just then, there was no telling what further humiliation Myeong-chol might have been made to suffer. The security officer glanced out of the window, then picked up the telephone receiver.

"Military security operations division? A vehicle just arrived. Yes, yes. I'll send them all to you."

He put the receiver down and began to herd the people out of the hut.

"Come on, move, the lot of you!"

"*Aigo*, Officer, Comrade!"

"Please sir, my son's father-in-law passed away, he only lives in the next village. . . ."

"I did have my papers with me, I swear it, but I lost them on the way, ..."

In the midst of this hive of commotion, Myeong-chol seized the officer's arm.

"Comrade Officer!"

For someone like Myeong-chol, awkward and indecisive by nature, this was an act of quite extraordinary bravery, going far beyond anything he had ever dared before. But he was forced to it, by the memory of all the trials he'd had to battle just to get here, and by the urgent voice inside his head reminding him of how his mother must be suffering, clinging painfully to life in the hope of a final reunion with her son.

To have come all this way only to be turned around and sent packing before even setting foot in his childhood home was simply unbearable.

"Please, Comrade Officer, consider my situation!"

"What the hell do you think you're doing?" the officer barked, snatching his arm away. He glared at Myeong-chol as though he were a piece of trash offending him by its very presence. "The crows can caw all they like, but you shut your mouth! You deserve to be thrown into prison, do you hear me?"

But even that ghastly word "prison" could not intimidate Myeong-chol now. He would pay any price, run any risk, to see his mother one last time. What did it matter then if they jailed him? It would be like being hit in a dream.

But it was not to be. The sentry with the gun came running over, and the whole group, Myeong-chol included, was forced up into the truck, like pigs being sent to the slaughterhouse. There were no exceptions, not for the old woman who clung to the officer's ankle, not for the bent-backed man who walked with a cane. The truck roared into life, belching out a round of black exhaust fumes as it shunted forward.

Mother!

Myeong-chol's breath rasped in his throat. His eyes grew misty, and when the old ferry came into view he couldn't hold back his tears. He pitied his poor mother, waiting in vain for a stupid, good-for-nothing son, and he grieved at his own cruel fate, which had him stuck like a fly in a web.

Mother! Forgive me. Your idiot son, your idiot son . . .

An opaque cloud of dust billowed up in the wake of the truck, obliterating the fields and mountains of his home. A moment ago he could have reached out and touched them; now, he might as well have been separated from them by a distance of ten thousand _ri_.

Their son had woken up and begun to grizzle. Myeong-chol lapsed into silence, taking a few more drags on his cigarette. It was the first he'd smoked since returning home, after the past few days recovering from his ordeal, and it was making his head spin. Jeongsuk shook herself.

"Look, Yeong-min, your dad's awake! Here, look. Look at your son!"

"Son? Ha!" Myeong-chol's laugh was strained. Though he could see that Jeongsuk was trying to put on a brave face, adopting a deliberately bright tone that did not match her puffy eyes, he seemed unable, or at least unwilling, to do the same.

"Yeong-min, you're happy to see your dad, aren't you, hey?" Jeongsuk bravely battled on, tickling their son under the chin.

"What good is a son in this country of ours? When a mother is lying on her deathbed, and her son can't even show his face? Sons!"

"Don't be like that, please. It's done with now, there's no use going back over it. You'll apply again for a permit, and this time it's bound to be approved. Your mother's health will hold out that long, I'm sure of it."

As much as Jeongsuk wanted to support her husband, the account of his ordeals had left her badly shaken, and she naturally tried to bury the memory with these words of empty comfort. *After all,* she thought, *wounds never heal if you keep tearing them open.* But there was one rather more pressing worry that she felt she needed to get off her chest.

"But what's going to happen about your job? You've been absent without leave for over twenty days. . . ."

"Ah," Myeong-chol said with a strange smile, "but I have a good reason. One that even the factory won't be able to argue with."

He picked up the notebook that was lying on the desk, extracted a folded slip of paper from between its pages, and handed it Jeongsuk. She read it through hastily.

Name: Kim Myeong-chol
    Confirmation that the above-named comrade will undertake labor discipline for the period stated below, as penalty for violating travel regulations.
From 2nd July 1992 to 24th July 1992.
South Pyongan Province, Military Security Department Labor Discipline Office

"No!" This cry escaped from between Jeongsuk's lips as she wrenched her gaze from the note to her husband.

This time it was Myeong-chol's turn to adopt a cheerful tone.

"As you said, what's done is done, right? And it was only twenty-two days, after all. Twenty-two days I had to spend as an ox, muzzled and bridled."

"Don't—don't tell me any more," Jeongsuk shouted, clamping her hands over her ears. She pictured the bruises and welts her husband's shirt must be concealing, remembered the lice-infested underwear she'd had to wash. Her chest ached.

Outside the window, a skylark cried, and Myeong-chol sat up in surprise. Turning to the window, he saw the cage hanging from the eaves, just as it had always used to.

"How can that be?"

"The very next morning after you set them free, they came flying right back again. So I put them back in their cage."

"Pitiful, domesticated creatures!" Myeong-chol muttered as though chewing and spitting each word.

The larks chirped again as though to counter Myeong-chol. He could imagine what they might be saying: "Aren't you just the same? You came back too, after all. . . ."

That's right, what am I but a caged animal, for whom the shortest distance might as well be a thousand ri? *A pitiful, domesticated creature!*

Myeong-chol sprang to his feet. The line of his lips looked firm as a rock, while a raised rope of muscle pulsed over one cheek. He leaned outside the window and unhooked the cage, holding it out at arm's length. Something like a moan leaked from his mouth. With oddly unhurried motions, and as though operating independently of his body, each hand began to wrench at its side of the cage. There was a loud crack, and the cage split in two. Calmly and without hesitating, as though he had rehearsed all these movements, Myeong-chol let the two halves clatter to the floor. The larks turned a single circle inside the room, then darted out of the window swift as arrows.

"Why did you do that?" Jeongsuk's voice quavered with fear; she had never known her husband to behave like this.

"There's no 'why.' I needed to break the cage, so I did, that's all."

As Myeong-chol gazed quietly at the larks enjoying their freedom, his face was eerily self-possessed. From outside, there came the sound of footsteps and the rustling of paper, and then a postal worker thrust a telegram in through the open window. Myeong-chol and Jeongsuk both reached out to take it, and their eyes fell on those four small characters, gouging into them like a knife into a gut.

"MOTHER DECEASED."

There was no wailing, no sobbing, no falling to the floor. The two hands holding the telegram merely trembled, silently, shaken by something far more powerful than tears.

7th February, 1993

Pandemonium

On the mountain behind the village, a cuckoo crowed, crying out as if it were choking on a clot of blood. So Mrs. Oh wasn't the only one for whom sleep was proving impossible.

The drawn-out sigh her husband made spoke of his own discomfort. Then, as though it was a chain reaction, their granddaughter started up crying.

"Baby, does it hurt?"

Mrs. Oh's trembling hand fumbled in the darkness for her granddaughter's bandaged leg. Her fingers bumped up against a squared-off wooden board, hard and chill to the touch. A shiver ran down her spine.

Though she tried to sigh out the ache inside her, it remained stubbornly lodged in her chest. Her five-year-old granddaughter's broken leg was obviously painful, but Mrs. Oh had her own sufferings to contend with, the bandage around her lower back forcing her to lie rigid in the same uncomfortable position. A few days ago, when the elderly couple had visited their pregnant daughter, whose due date was fast approaching, they'd thought that by bringing the little girl home with them for a spell they were doing a good deed, allowing the mother to focus on taking care of herself. If Mrs. Oh could have foreseen that such a calamity would befall the child . . .

"Mama . . ."

"Little Yeongsun. Now that your leg's better, let's go and take the train to see Mum, hey?"

"Don't want to, don't want to, don't want to go on the train . . ."

Her whimpered cries, which up until now had been as faint as the sound of a trickling stream, exploded into a full-blown howl. Shredding the dark interior of the house to pieces, the sound was one of despair and protest.

"What are you doing, mentioning that awful train in front of the child? It's enough to give anyone the shivers," Mrs. Oh's husband complained. The child's cries doubled in volume, as though her grandfather's remarks had swelled her sorrow even further.

"Oh, of course," Mrs. Oh muttered, "I'm a foolish old woman, it's true." She got up and searched for the light switch. Once the room had brightened, she moved to embrace the tearful girl.

"Eh, our little Yeongsun, will you give Grandma a hug?" Overwhelming pity swelled up inside her and she slid her arms beneath her granddaughter's body, being careful of her bandaged leg, and lifted her up. Carrying the little girl in her arms, she went over to the window bench where she'd spent the past few hours, and sat back down again.

> Feel better, feel better
> Our little one's hurt
> Let your nice grandma
> Soothe it for you. . . .

Though Mrs. Oh made every effort to comfort the child in her lap, the little girl was unable to quell her tears. Her sorrow seemed not to have subsided at all, so deeply had it pierced her innocent self. How to undo the hurt inside her, how to heal the wound inflicted when her soft knee had snapped, like the sparrow who fell afoul of evil Nolbu?

"Yeongsun, your grandma made a mistake." The words seemed to split Mrs. Oh's throat in two. "We won't take the train again, okay? Never again!"

Never! There it was again, that hellish din, ringing in her ears as though reminding her to keep this promise. And that dreadful train station, the source of the commotion, appearing in her mind's eye like a scene from some nightmare . . .

"There are people dying here!" screamed Mrs. Oh, seized by the despairing conviction that she was about to breathe her last, buried in this jumble of people. Her head and back were being steadily crushed by this mass of contorted, entangled limbs, while heavy blows knocked the wind from her chest. Throbbing heat, the stink of sweat, the gooey mud under her feet . . . these things were already growing faint for her, receding into the background. Only one single thought hung clear and sharp in her mind—that this was how she was going to die. Perhaps it was all her long years as a history teacher that gave her the illusion, now, of being caught up in a mass of starving slaves, in one of the grain riots she'd taught her pupils about.

And Mrs. Oh would have truly met her end in that spot, were it not for the fact that the bread supplies ran out just in the nick of time. As soon as all the bread from the handcart was sold, the maelstrom subsided. Mrs. Oh managed to buy three packs just before the chaos reached fever pitch, and kept them clutched safe to her chest the whole time. Holding in her mind the thought that they had been bought with their last ration coupons, that without them the family would go hungry for however long it now took to make it to their destination, Mrs. Oh kept a tight grip on these precious packets.

"Hey! Even grandmothers are crawling around in this mess?" a sweat-soaked young man cried in surprise when he spotted Mrs. Oh. Concentrating on finding her other shoe, which had come off and got kicked away from her in the melee, she gave no sign of having heard him. She found the muddied shoe and put it on, but there still remained the task of getting back into the waiting room to rejoin her husband and granddaughter. The room was rammed to the gills, so much so that even the window frames had disappeared, gotten rid of in a bid to free up some space. Whatever had previously been a window was now used as a door, and the water bottles people had brought with them for the journey were transformed into chamber pots. If only it could have just stopped raining, they wouldn't all have had to cram into such a tiny space. But as it was, the waiting room was their only refuge against getting soaked to the skin.

People lying down or sitting on the concrete floor, in spite of all the mud that had got trailed in from outside; people lacking even the space to sit, who instead had to stand stiff as posts—almost all of them were people who, like Mrs. Oh and her family, had been intending to change trains here at this station, only to find themselves imprisoned because a Class One event was being held.

The station itself wasn't particularly large and was far away from any built-up areas, but it was one at which various branch lines converged, meaning that even a small change in the service was enough to cause a severe backlog. That would have been bad enough in itself, but as the station had now been completely locked down for thirty-two hours and counting, crowds and confusion were only to be expected. The would-be passengers had all exhausted whatever provisions they'd brought for the journey, and the scant handful of basic restaurants were unable to meet their demands. Even buying a packet of bread involved the kind of ordeal which Mrs. Oh had just suffered through, and the difficulties in then getting back to the waiting room were no less of a strain. People's nerves were on edge, leading them to kick up a fuss over the least perceived slight. Faces blackened with dust from the railroad were screwed up in irritation; people grumbled that someone had jogged the backpack they were using as a pillow or had elbowed them in the ribs while shoving past. And even when these petty spats had run out of steam, the same angry expression remained on everyone's face.

What bastard's Class One event takes this long? What bastard's Class One event kills people like this? Of course, these words of discontent could never pass their lips. The Class One event taking place just then involved Kim Il-sung traveling along that same railroad—Kim Il-sung, whose sacred inviolability meant that even if he announced that a convicted murderer was to be allowed to live, anyone who dared so much as hint at disapproval would be sealing his or her own fate, with no more recourse to reverse it than a mouse faced with a cat. Indeed, the "cats" would be all around the station just now, even inside the waiting room, scattered among the mice like the seeds in a squash.

In all likelihood, the cats would pretend to share the sufferings of the mice right next to them, even producing the same pitiful whimpers whenever they happened to be bumped or jolted . . . and the wretched mice, suspecting this, could only divert their anger onto the most trivial incidents, like the bride who takes it out on the family dog when her mother-in-law gives her a tongue-lashing.

With so many people looking for the family dog in this situation, it took Mrs. Oh a full ten minutes to get back to the place where her husband and granddaughter were waiting, though the distance from the yard in front of the station was no more than thirty-odd steps. The family had installed themselves in one corner of the waiting room, the ideal spot from which to avoid "attacks" from behind or to one side.

Yeongsun was the first to spot Mrs. Oh. "Bread!" she exclaimed.

They'd had to skip only one meal since setting out on their trip, yet the girl looked happier to see the bread than to see her grandmother. Her husband, though, was the same as always.

"Look at the sweat on you! That's why I said I should go. . . ."

He reached up to take a packet of bread and turned to the young woman who had borrowed Mrs. Oh's place. Her clothes marked her out as a recent bride. She had fallen asleep where she sat, her head lolling forward onto her backpack. "Excuse me, miss," he said to wake her, and shifted aside so she'd still have room now that Mrs. Oh was back. Tearing open her packet, Mrs. Oh held out a piece each to her husband and granddaughter.

"I'm all right," the old man said, pretending not to be hungry, though in truth he was holding back. Before Mrs. Oh had gone out to the yard, he'd given her the last ration coupon from his wallet. Each packet it had bought contained five small pieces, fifteen all told—and this was all they had to last them until they reached their destination.

"Go on, eat. Don't worry about the child. The train will set off any moment now, you'll see. Do you really think they'd

127

let us starve to death here?" Mrs. Oh forced a piece of bread into her husband's hand.

"Well then, you have some too."

As it seemed the only way to get her husband to follow suit, Mrs. Oh took a bite of their precious stash. In reality, the couple were both on edge, worried that the little they had wasn't going to last and Yeongsun would end up going hungry.

"Wow! You look like you're enjoying that. . . ."

The young woman who had given her place to Mrs. Oh, and who was now sitting crammed up against them, laughed at the sight of sweet-faced Yeongsun devouring her bread in great gulps.

"Ah, what was I thinking? Here, have a piece." Genuinely apologetic, Mrs. Oh handed the packet of bread to the young woman.

"Yes, have one," her husband insisted.

"No, no," the young woman said, firmly pushing the packet back and smiling warmly at the couple's concern. "I have some food of my own in my backpack. But have you got far to go? After all this . . ."

"Oh, we've come a fair way already, but there's not much farther left now. As long as we can get out of this awful situation . . ."

"For goodness' sake, when on earth will this train—oh!" The young woman moaned abruptly, seemingly taken by surprise. Both hands instinctively went to her lower stomach, and she buried her face in her backpack.

"Are you all right?" Mrs. Oh asked. "But of course—you must be expecting." Perhaps it was due to embarrassment, or perhaps simply because of the pain, but in any case the young woman couldn't manage an answer. Mrs. Oh decided to be more direct. "How many months?"

"Eight . . . Everything was fine, but I got jostled in the crowd just now, trying to get my ticket stamped. . . ."

"Whatever can we do?" Mrs. Oh exclaimed. "Here in the middle of nowhere . . ." Her anxiety was genuine, as much as if the problem concerned her own family. Why, this woman could have been her own daughter, whose pregnancy was similarly advanced. In this day and age, when young women found it every bit as tough as men to get by, who could say that some similar calamity hadn't befallen her own daughter in the few days since they'd seen her last?

"Here, make yourself comfortable." His own thoughts in tune with his wife's, the old man tucked his legs in to give the woman a little more space.

"Oh my . . ."

But as for what happened to her after that, there was no way for any of them to know. No sooner had the old man encouraged her to lie down than a rumor sprang up that tickets were finally being checked for anyone traveling north, and the waiting room suddenly sprang into action. The upheaval was so great that by the time it subsided, the entire place had gotten so topsy-turvy that complete strangers now found themselves practically in each other's laps. But though the young woman herself had disappeared, the thought of her plight continued to haunt Mrs. Oh, strengthening her resolve that something must be done.

When she'd found out about her own daughter's pregnancy, one of the first things she did was to send a letter to her younger brother, who lived far away in the mountains, asking him if he could get his hands on a wild boar's gallbladder. Everyone knew boars' bladders were packed with nutrients and were just the thing to help a woman get her strength back after childbirth.

Her brother's home was only four stations away from the one they were currently stranded at, back in the direction they'd come from. Surely she could walk that far. . . . And with one mouth less to feed, the four ration coupons would last so much longer! This wasn't the first time Mrs. Oh had had such thoughts. Just now, when her husband had handed her the final coupon, she'd sounded him out upon the matter, only to be roundly scolded. But now, with the young woman's fate a clear warning in her mind, her intention had grown firm. There was no space for hesitation.

"Yeongsun's grandfather! There's nothing else for it; I have to go through with my plan."

"Ah, you're not back on that again?" Her husband had been sitting awkwardly hunched over their sleeping granddaughter, trying to shield her from the jostling crowd. Now, he straightened up and looked his wife in the face.

"I have to do this. Have you forgotten that young woman already?"

"Pfft! Forgotten, indeed!"

"If a woman meets with an accident in childbirth, she can suffer from the effects her whole life. Her whole life!"

" . . . "

"I've thought it through, and this is the best way. We can kill two birds with one stone. Please, you'll say yes?"

"Oh, I've thought it through as well, you know. How can you expect to make it safely all that way? On your own, and at your age."

"Well, don't you worry yourself about that."

Eventually, Mrs. Oh got ready to set out. But when it came down to it, parting from her husband and granddaughter felt uncomfortably like leaving them to fend for themselves in a patch of thorns. Her feet were like lead as she took the first step. Slowly, constantly turning to look back, Mrs. Oh began to walk away from that station waiting room, which would remain seared on her memory like a brand.

As the child on her lap resumed her soft weeping, Mrs. Oh was pulled back to the present.

Though Yeongsun's sobbing had now died down, the sense of fate's cruelty that had grown up inside her was apparently refusing to disperse. With a trembling hand, Mrs. Oh stroked the soft, downy hairs by the girl's face. Even her husband hadn't escaped unscathed from the chaos at the station; that was how serious it was. But there would have been nothing she could have done even if she'd stayed behind.

All the same, she couldn't help reproaching herself. She might fall to her knees in front of her granddaughter and beg the girl's forgiveness, but even that wouldn't entirely get rid of her guilt, her feeling that she, who called herself Yeong-sun's grandmother, had brought the child to this sorry state by running away when she needed her most. Of course, the child's injury was nothing compared with what her husband suffered, his pelvis twisted badly out of joint. But the girl was just a tender young bud, in the springtime of her life! Even more than the damage to her leg, which had to be encased in a stiff bandage, the fear and agitation this suffering had caused were surely deserving of pity.

"How about another of Grandma's old stories, Yeong-sun?" It was impossible for Mrs. Oh not to try to comfort her granddaughter, to make up for the pain she felt she'd caused, in whatever small way she could. The girl merely nodded in answer.

"Right then, let me see. Once upon a time on a certain seashore . . ."

"There lived a kind old fisherman, right? You already told me that one. Back at home."

"Ah, so I did! In that case . . . I've got it. Once upon a time there was a merchant who sold pots . . ."

"Who was scurrying down the road with his pots on his back . . . Hee-hee . . ." It appeared that Yeongsun had forgotten her pain, at least for this little while. "You told me the pot merchant story too. The same day."

Mrs. Oh was lost for words. All of a sudden, she felt as though her heart were wandering in a distant field, leaving behind only her mumbling mouth, trying and failing to think of another story.

"Hoho . . . Seeing our Yeongsun laughing with Grandma has made this old man's pain all better." Her husband was lying rigid as ever, his eyes boring into the ceiling. His warm affection was palpable in the unusual softness with which he spoke; to Mrs. Oh, it was clearly an attempt to make her see that her granddaughter bore her no grudge whatsoever.

"Quickly, Grandma."

"Yes, yes, it's coming to me now." But though Mrs. Oh had found her voice, she didn't seem able to produce another tale, so moved was she by the depth of her husband's affection.

"Looks like you've used up all your grandma's stories, Yeongsun! How about one from me instead?"

"Okay." Yeongsun's cheerful, matter-of-fact answer showed how utterly ignorant she was of the effort this was costing her grandfather.

"Cock-a-doodle-do, do you know the one about the rooster, Yeongsun?"

It was this that finally moved Mrs. Oh to tears: her husband imitating a rooster's call, an attempt to help their granddaughter recover her child's innocence, in which she too could detect a plaintive note. The more strenuous his efforts, intended to assuage his wife's guilty conscience even more than to lighten their granddaughter's heart, the less

Mrs. Oh found herself able to conceal her emotions. All this for her sake!

He was a teacher at the same middle school as his wife, and his lessons were known to be tough and rigorous, but pupils and close acquaintances alike received great affection from him, and gave nothing but love and respect in return.

Cuckoo, cuckoo.

Midnight had passed, and the cuckoo still didn't know how to quit. . . . That sound stitched the nighttime stillness, punctuating Mr. Oh's telling of Aesop's fable, in a pain-filled voice. . . .

Even if I hadn't left the station that day, perhaps this kind of calamity . . .

Against her wishes, Mrs. Oh's thoughts once again turned back to the event of a few days ago, which she could not shake from her mind.

Only once Mrs. Oh had left the station and made it onto the newly constructed highway did she realize that it, too, was caught up in the Class One event. The road seemed to play hide-and-seek with the railroad, the former hugging the coast while the latter sometimes ducked away inland. And the road was utterly deserted; no vehicle dared to cast a shadow there, much less individuals on foot. All traffic had met a blockade farther up; Mrs. Oh had managed to smuggle herself on only by coming via the station. What on earth was this Class One event, if both road and rail traffic had to be suspended? Were there two Kim Il-sungs paying a visit? One thing was for sure: There would be "cats" stationed at each key point on the route.

And indeed, Mrs. Oh was stopped and questioned four times before she'd even gone fifteen *ri*. Aware that her age was her only shield, each time she tried to use it to her full advantage. How could she have done otherwise? How could she be frank or sincere when there was no knowing what might happen if she let her guard down? Using wiles that she'd never known she possessed, she even feigned a touch of deafness, repeating "Yes? Yes?" when in reality she could hear perfectly well. She was just an old woman going to that village over there, yes, just over there, why, she was practically there already. ID? What ID were they talking about?

She dragged out her griping as though this were all just some terrible inconvenience. A few times they glared down their noses at her as though she were a criminal, while at others, though their speech and actions were kind, their wildcat eyes would rake her up and down, striking a chill into her heart. Each time, though, presumably judging that Mrs. Oh was unlikely to be a criminal mastermind intending to plant a bomb, nor a crack-shot sniper planning to conceal herself in the woods, they would eventually tell her to be on her way, adding a raft of warnings before she'd even had time to obey:

"But go along by the side of the road, not on it, and as soon as you hear a vehicle, no matter how far off it sounds, get out of sight. Understand?"

"Yes, yes."

Having made it through those four rounds of questioning, Mrs. Oh was picking her way along the stony road that lay between the railroad and the sea and dealing with intermittent bursts of rain when from behind her came the blare of a car horn. Glancing back, she saw a convoy of black cars moving along the new highway; the dense stand of pines that screened the highway from the sea must have kept her from hearing the vehicles' approach.

Mrs. Oh was utterly horrified, and dashed off the road. Up until almost that point, she'd been careful to keep off the road itself, mindful of the cats' orders, struggling along instead on the verge, where her feet kept getting caught in grass thickets or slipping into the churned earth of the paddy fields. But then she had reached a point where there was no verge to walk on, neither on the railroad side nor on the coast side, so there'd been nothing else for it but to get back on the road.

Why did these extraordinary vehicles have to be overtaking her here, of all places? Mrs. Oh's heart began to pound, anticipating an imminent crisis. Two of the cars had already swept past her when a whistle shrilled in her ears. She whipped her head around automatically, and her field of vision was instantly filled by a long line of cars stretching into the distance. She jerked her gaze away, as though seeing something she ought not to, leapt across the ditch that bordered the road, and fled into the pine wood. But the sound of a car door opening, and the voice that followed it, stopped her flight as effectively as a hand seizing her ankle would have.

"Grandma, the Great Leader, Father of Us All, wants to see you."

Mrs. Oh turned around. Her head felt heavy and dull, as though a blunt blow had struck her on the back of her skull, and everything grew dark in front of her eyes.

"No, no . . ." she muttered repeatedly, barely aware of what she was doing, pawing the air in front of her chest as though trying to push something away. Her vision gradually cleared, and the person facing her began to pull into focus. The man, whose clothes and general appearance were as flawless as a rod of steel, slipped his fingers lightly around Mrs. Oh's wrist, his expression one of amusement.

"Come along."

Under this man's guidance, Mrs. Oh was brought, reeling, up to the parked car. She barely managed to keep control of her legs, which threatened to collapse beneath her and dump her on the ground. The men standing around the car were as neat and smart as the first, equally calm and collected.

Among them, though, one stood out, a dignified figure shielded by the open car door. A man whose pale golden clothes seemed to shed a soft veil of mist, enveloping him from his shoes to his fedora; a man who was gazing in Mrs. Oh's direction from behind gleaming dark brown lenses; a man who was unmistakably "the Great Leader, Father of Us All, Kim Il-sung," a visage Mrs. Oh had known all her life, though only ever as one that gazed out at her from portraits or the television. His bulging paunch bent his arms into the shape of the Cyrillic letter ф,while the face that rose above, perhaps enjoying the refreshing sea breeze through the pines, perhaps amused by the sight of the diminutive Mrs. Oh tottering forward and held by the wrist as though she might fly away, was beaming.

Feeling as though her body had suddenly withered to the size of a dried jujube, Mrs. Oh dropped to her knees about five paces in front of Kim Il-sung. As she did, words slid as smoothly from her mouth as a coiled spring being released.

"I respectfully pray for the long life of our Great Leader, Father of Us All."

No matter who you were, if you lived in this land, beneath these skies, you would have memorized these words time and time again ever since you learned to speak; hence they flowed without a hitch even from Mrs. Oh's mouth.

"Oh, thank you." This cheerful voice came from somewhere above Mrs. Oh's head. "Adjutant, get her up. Up!"

The man grasped Mrs. Oh's arms and raised her up. Several other men got out of their parked cars and gathered around.

"Where are you going on foot like this?" Kim Il-sung's voice rang with deep sympathy.

Tape recorders whirred and cameras flashed. Filming equipment clicked and clacked in all directions. All this left Mrs. Oh even more flustered, but she fought to steady her wits and answer Kim Il-sung's question. Briefly, her mind fumbling for the right words, she informed her superior of her situation—though, of course, she did not forget to conceal that the root cause of all her woes was the present Class One event.

"Ah, I see." Kim Il-sung smiled broadly at Mrs. Oh's answer, his head bobbing as vigorously as a mortar pounding grain. "If this boar's bladder is all you're in search of, we can take you in our car straight to your daughter's house. We were going in that direction anyway."

"Oh no, no, I couldn't possibly, Great Leader!"

"You don't need to worry about your daughter. We will help her get to the maternity hospital in Pyongyang."

"No, but I couldn't, something like that, for the likes of me . . ."

"It's no trouble. I too am a son of the people. Just the thought of past days pains me, when our people had to walk everywhere on foot; why should they walk now, when all the conditions are in place to ensure a pleasant journey? Come, ride with us."

Mrs. Oh was truly stumped; to ride in the same car as Kim Il-sung would put her utterly out of her wits, but to refuse would be discourteous. But then someone came to her rescue—a curly-haired man standing by the car to the rear of Kim Il-sung's, a flat briefcase tucked under his arm.

"Great Leader, it seems riding in the same car as yourself might be a little too much for this humble grandmother; I'll follow along with her in mine."

"That seems like a good idea," the steel rod said approvingly.

"Really? Well, perhaps that will set the old woman's mind at ease. In that case, Grandmother, come along in the car behind."

No sooner had Kim Il-sung finished speaking than he put his hand on Mrs. Oh's back and gave her a gentle push in the direction of the other car, still beaming at her all the while. Mrs. Oh herself could not have said how she ended up installed in the car, after another round of flashing and clicking which the curly-haired man guided her through. The scenery beyond the car window, whose glass had seemed black from outside, was brighter and more animated than Mrs. Oh could have imagined, like the world looked at from underwater. It seemed as though her whole body would sink into the soft, yielding seat.

Some faint scent, redolent of luxury, hung in the car's interior. The background music was as discreet as that scent, barely there, and with no hint as to where it was coming from. Mrs. Oh couldn't even tell when they began to move. The car's passage was so smooth it seemed to glide over the ground. It was like a dream. To have been plucked from the thorny path that had been her life so far, and placed in such unexpected splendor! And she wasn't the only one—now they were telling her that her daughter would be able to give birth in Pyongyang's maternity hospital. How could such a thing be possible, unless it was a dream?

"How are you feeling, Grandma?" said the curly-haired man, smiling and turning to look back from the front passenger seat.

"Well, you know, I would have been fine just walking. . . . I really don't want to be putting you out."

"Never mind that, just sit there comfortably and enjoy your journey, as the Great Leader said. Our convoy will accompany the train until we stop being able to see the coast. But the Great Leader has said that this car is to take you right to your daughter's door."

"No, but surely . . . not on my account."

"Grandma! Is it not higher than the heavens and deeper than the seas, the Great Leader's love?"

"Yes, of course," Mrs. Oh replied, giving several deep bows. For a short while afterward, she struggled to remember what it was she had just agreed to. The car was speeding along. Pine trees and telegraph poles whisked past the windows in twin columns, like guards lining a processional route.

They had been traveling for around twenty minutes when it happened. A steam whistle sounded, and a glorious train procession appeared to the car's left. Mrs. Oh had never seen a train like it, with white curtains at each window and each door shining as dazzlingly as the long roof. She recalled the curly-haired man saying that the train would be used when the route ducked away from the coast. This was the special train that Kim Il-sung, riding in the car at the head of the convoy, would now transfer into. Only now was Mrs. Oh able to grasp just what kind of Class One event could shut down both road and rail. Kim Il-sung was traveling along a route where both options were possible, so they took the train when that was most convenient, then switched to the car whenever there was an opportunity to enjoy the coastal scenery. . . .

"Ah! Whichever way you look at it, it's best to travel by train," the curly-haired man muttered to himself, pleased to catch sight of this mode of transport. Mrs. Oh was equally gladdened by the sight, as it meant that ordinary trains would now be able to pass through the branch station. But that happiness was fleeting. As soon as the special train's long tail had vanished from sight, leaving great reverberations in its wake, a ghastly vision appeared in front of Mrs. Oh's eyes—the uproar of that station waiting room, where a bomb had seemed to go off at the sound of the first ticket inspection!

Worn out by the rain and the waiting and the hunger, people now at the point of madness surge out through the door and windows in a great tide. The narrow passage between the ticket inspection windows transforms into a sea of people. Screams come from all sides; people push and shove, no longer caring about their tickets, just struggling to extricate themselves from each other's flailing limbs, walls creaking as they fight forward. . . .

Mrs. Oh catches sight of her husband's white head, only for it vanish back into the melee. She spots him again—he has Yeongsun on his back. He is waving one arm. Finally, she sees him suffer the same fate as the rice scoop that falls into the boiling vat of porridge! Screams and shouts . . .

"Yeongsun!" Mrs. Oh cries out. Startled, she jerks awake from her vision. Seeing that no one else in the car is paying her any attention, she guesses that no words have actually passed her lips. The car's quiet burr as it rolls along the road kindles a sweet languor within its walls.

Mrs. Oh's reminiscence was abruptly dispelled by her husband's calling her name. "Is the child asleep?" the old man asked, unable to sit up and look for himself. Mrs. Oh looked down at the girl in her lap.

"Yes, she's asleep."

"Ah, so I was telling that story to myself, then!"

"Thank you, anyway. Now you should get some rest too."

"You think I can sleep in my condition?"

"Oh, and to think that while you and that child were going through hell, this stupid old woman was sitting in a comfortable car . . ."

"There's no need to keep going back over that. Would you have preferred all three of us to suffer? There's no point to those 'if onlys.'"

"*Aigo*, when will the two of you be fit and well again?"

"Wait!" The old man pricked up his ears. "Is that your voice?"

Knowing only too well the cause of his surprise, Mrs. Oh stayed where she was. Yes, it was her voice—ringing out from the loudspeaker at the edge of the village.

And so I ended up being ushered over to a car parked on the new highway. And next to the car was the Great Leader himself, Father of Us All. . . .

These were the words which Mrs. Oh had dutifully mouthed four days previously. Alighting from the car that day, she'd been desperate for news of her husband and granddaughter, but had been greeted instead by a swarm of journalists. So persistently did they hold their microphones up, she had no choice but to open her mouth. The result had been broadcast on both radio and television for the past two days, but this was the first time her husband had gotten to hear it, as he'd made it home only the previous evening, after stints first at the railroad and then at the military hospitals. He'd been told about it by Mrs. Oh, but hearing it for himself was a different matter; no wonder he was surprised.

He was straining to hear, afraid of missing a single syllable. Mrs. Oh's face flushed as if someone had discovered her doing something untoward. If only a hole could have opened up she would have hidden herself in it then and there; even a mouse hole would have done! Her voice booming out of the loudspeaker was like a blade picking at the wounds of her husband and Yeongsun. How could it seem any other way, with her bragging about her own good fortune when two people she loved had spent those selfsame hours in a hellish situation, a pandemonium, which might well have been their end?

Mrs. Oh wished the broadcast would hurry up and end. How many days had it been already . . . and still the loudspeaker jabbered on and on, until the whole world must surely have had its message rammed into their ears.

The Great Leader had me ride in the car the whole way—he wouldn't set off again until I agreed.

Eventually, her speech ran its course. Now it was the turn of the feverish broadcaster to add insult to injury.

"Do you hear this, listeners? These words of boundless gratitude toward our Great Leader, toward our socialist system! Such is the love our Great Leader holds for us, a pleasant route has now been opened so that our people can travel free

144

from discomfort under these skies and beside this sea, and happy laughter rings out all along that route, like that of this old woman, Oh Chun-hwa."

Run on, run on, train, run on
The whistle sounds a note of love. . . .

"Aahhh!" Her husband's high-pitched moan abruptly drowned out the broadcast, echoing inside the room.

Cuckoo, cuckoo . . .

The cuckoo had stayed silent for a while, but now its call broke out again. Mrs. Oh fancied that the sound was coming out of her husband's chest, a clot of blood being coughed up which was all the anguish he couldn't put into words. How could such agony fail to bite deeply, the pain of having to watch with his own eyes as his hip bone and his granddaughter's leg were broken? To say nothing of that pain now being recklessly aggravated by the broadcaster's boast of the "pleasant route"!

Yesterday, when her husband and Yeongsun had been transported home from the hospital, he had told Mrs. Oh in minute detail all they had suffered at the station. Based on his account, the vision that sprang up in her mind while she was riding in the car had been no illusion, but almost an exact mirror of reality. The only ways in which it didn't quite tally were that the walls of the ticket barriers were not pushed out—though four of the gates did collapse—and that the pair had been buried in the tide of humanity with Yeongsun not on her grandfather's back but clutched tightly to his chest.

How on earth would the pregnant young woman have fared in such a free-for-all, with her stomach already paining her? And those three could not have been the only victims, the only ones to have their limbs snapped, to have their hips twisted, to end up having a miscarriage. . . .

But those cries of pain which, if combined, would be enough to cause even hell to overflow, had all disappeared somewhere, drowned out by the sound of "happy laughter"— apparently swelled by Mrs. Oh herself! Laughter produced by one who had had the fingernails of both hands ripped off! Were such things possible in this world? How could the screams and cries of such a mass of people be transformed into "happy laughter" without a cruel sorcery being at work?

Mrs. Oh shuddered. All of a sudden the image of a demon working just such black magic flashed in front of her eyes. Some ancient, hugely corpulent demon which conducted itself extremely freely. Having dexterously whipped up the magic which had created that "happy laughter," it was now waddling busily back and forth preparing a similar spell. Only this time, the object would be not Mrs. Oh herself but her daughter, who had given birth in the maternity hospital.

Mrs. Oh shuddered again. So far, thanks to that demon's sorcery, the people of this land had been living lives turned entirely on their heads, utterly different from the truth.

Yeongsun's shrill voice, which was making noises as though she was fending something off, snapped Mrs. Oh right back to her senses. But the child on her lap was just mumbling in her sleep, her breathing an even ebb and flow.

Mrs. Oh thought she must be dreaming, perhaps reliving the moment when her leg had snapped.

"Is she sleep-talking?" Her husband seemed likewise to have been busy with his own thoughts, only for the girl's voice to jolt him out of them.

"Yes, that's all it is. She's settled down now. . . . You try to get yourself some sleep." Mrs. Oh wished she could give him some comfort, some relief from his aching, smarting thoughts. "Why keep tormenting yourself, it's all done with now. . . ."

"What? I wasn't thinking about that at all," her husband said. "I'm not bothered about any old broadcast. . . . I was just thinking about what story to tell the girl when she wakes up."

That was the kind of man he was. Caring more for his wife's distress than his own, he refused to admit to being racked with painful thoughts, seeking instead to veil his own suffering with whatever it might comfort her to believe. Nor did Mrs. Oh intend to strip away that veil. If nothing else, it might help ease that torturous night for both of them.

"You're right—when she wakes up she'll be begging for another story. I've never known a child to be so rapt when she's listening to something!" Mrs. Oh said.

"It's lucky there's something that can ease things for her."

"In any case, don't worry. I've got an old tale up my sleeve."

"Hoho . . . Pushkin again?"

"No. The story of Pandemonium this time."

"Pandemonium? The abode of the demons?" her husband asked.

"Yes. Would you like me to tell it to you first?"

"Ha . . . I'm not Yeongsun."

"Yeongsun isn't the only one who could do with something to ease her pain." Mrs. Oh couldn't make it through this remark without a lump rising to her throat.

"I'll play Yeongsun, then." Nor was her husband's answer free from such evident emotion. Just about managing to control her trembling voice, Mrs. Oh embarked on the story she'd been planning.

"Once upon a time there was a garden, surrounded on all sides by a great, high fence. In that garden, an old demon ruled over thousands upon thousands of slaves. But the surprising thing was that the only sound ever to be heard within those high walls was the sound of merry laughter. Hahaha and hohoho, all year round—because of the laughing magic which the old demon used on his slaves.

"Why did he use such magic on them? To conceal his evil mistreatment of them, of course, and also to create a deception, saying, 'This is how happy the people in our garden are.' And that's also why he put the fences up, so that the people in other gardens couldn't see over or come in. So, well, think about it. Where in the world might you find such a garden, such a den of evil magic, where cries of pain and sadness were wrenched from the mouths of its people and distorted into laughter?"

Mrs. Oh began to choke up again, though she herself was not aware of it. The calculation she'd made when she began the tale, that it might offer just a brief moment of respite, had been misguided. The night had deepened; yet another bout of "happy laughter" was spilling out from the loudspeaker, casting into ever-starker relief the plot of that old tale, which was not really old at all.

30th December, 1995

On Stage

The mournful dirge flows out from the loudspeakers in a continuous stream, traveling slowly through the downtown streets where the rain keeps on falling. Its leaden cadence even filters into the meeting room of the municipal security department, adding further bleakness to the already subdued atmosphere.

To those gathered in the room, the announcers' voices seem unusually deep and clear, and they fancy that they see tears streaking down from the ceiling. The sound of the rain, the sound of the wind . . . Looking out beyond the window, its glass blurred by a solid stream of rainwater, they see the trailing tendrils of a gnarled old willow whipping through the air like a nest of snakes. When the wind pauses to gather its breath, its absence amplifies the sound of the rain, which pours down the roof in a plaintive *whoosh*.

All of these things taken together seemed an apt expression of our nation's mood, throwing the word "mourning" into stark relief. Those of us sitting here in the meeting seemed to be caught up somehow in a scene from a play, out of kilter with the real world.

The atmosphere of the meeting had built to a distressing tone, which caused us all to fall silent for a time. Now, when the director of the secret services, the Bowibu, shook himself and resumed his address, his voice sounded shrill and somewhat tinny in contrast to the measured, plaintive tone of the announcer.

"Now that every flower bed in this city has been stripped bare, now that we have risked poisonous snakes and landslides to bring further tribute from the fields and mountains, can we say that our Great Leader has been suitably mourned, sit back and rest assured of our loyalty? Absolutely not! Not when the very behavior we exist to stamp out has reared its ugly head within our own Bowibu family. In these tragic days, when even drowning ourselves in our own tears would not express the depth of our sorrow, there are those who sneak off to drink and flirt under the pretext of picking wildflowers!"

The Director, still clutching his tear-soaked handkerchief, brought his fist down on the lectern with such force he seemed to want to smash it to pieces. The wood shuddered in protest, and there was a perilous moment when the glass of water bouncing on its top seemed about to capsize.

"This point has already been emphasized, but you must remember that while our Great Leader's funeral is still in progress our agents must exercise the utmost vigilance, keeping their eyes and ears peeled at all times, their fists clenched and at the ready. And you must instill this necessity in them. Only then will we avoid falling victim to any further goblin trickery. I cannot stress this point enough. Well, that will be all for today."

The Director underlined his words by sharply clapping his journal closed, then followed that with a more restrained rap on the lectern. "Comrade Inspector for the Union of Enterprises, come to see me before you leave." This was spoken relatively quietly, but still loud enough to reach the ears of everyone in the room.

A stunted man sitting near the window turned to his bespectacled neighbor. "Did I hear right?" he murmured. "The Union of Enterprises?" His name was Hong Yeong-pyo, and his title was the very same that the Director had just called out. His neighbor nodded in confirmation, and Yeong-pyo abruptly felt several dozen gazes trained on him, as if he were caught in the beams of a battery of searchlights.

So it was you the Director was alluding to just now, when he said "within our own Bowibu family"! The message of those sharp eyes was loud and clear. As Yeong-pyo stepped forward, the words "to drink and flirt" echoed in his ears, and the face of his son Kyeong-hun swam queasily into his mind.

As soon as Yeong-pyo was standing in front of him, the Director waved a piece of paper in his face. "This came straight from one of our agents," he snapped, his voice stinging like a slap. *"'During the period of mourning for our Great*

Leader Comrade Kim Il-sung, Union of Enterprises employee Hong Kyeong-hun went to gather flowers in the foothills of Mount Baekryeon, where he was seen holding hands with factory girl Kim Suk-i—'"

"Kim Suk-i?" Yeong-pyo broke in, unable to restrain himself.

"That's not all! Holding hands, and also drinking alcohol. I have the evidence right here." He jerked his chin in the direction of a small plastic bottle on the desk next to Yeong-pyo. "It was still reeking when the agent brought it to me. Go on, smell for yourself."

But for Yeong-pyo, the issue was not one of alcohol. Kim Suk-i? Which Kim Suk-i? Surely not the elder girl, whom everyone called "Big Suk-i." Little Kim Suk-i, then? Let the Director be ignorant of that at least!

Luckily, the Director had a different interpretation of the horrified look on Yeong-pyo's face, imagining his subordinate to be aghast at the thought of having questioned his superior. "Quite right," he said, in a slightly softer tone, "the evidence of the report is perfectly sufficient. So what do you think, Comrade Hong: Can this be classed a general incident, or is it a political matter?"

"Of course it's political. Such behavior would be disgraceful at any time, but now! Now, when the inestimable loss of our Great Leader . . ." As though on cue, tears ran down Yeong-pyo's cheeks, sallow and sunken owing to a longstanding liver complaint. Even Yeong-pyo himself found it difficult to comprehend. How could the small cup of sadness sitting inside him produce a whole pitcher's worth of tears? But shedding them right now, in front of the Director, made them truly worth their weight in gold. . . .

"That'll do, that'll do." The Director, too, sounded somewhat choked, though he quickly recovered himself. "You know, Comrade Hong, the recommendation was to come down hard on this. But your feelings on the matter are clearly not to be faulted. You don't need me to explain the severity of the incident, and in any case, we went over all that in the meeting."

The Director softened his tone even further, sympathizing with this man who was so clearly ravaged by disease, and who was after all one of his own. "There won't be any official sanctions. I dealt with the report personally, as it concerned our Bowibu family. Go on, and take that bottle with you. Use it to bring your son to his senses."

"Thank you. Thank you." Bowing twice, Yeong-pyo left the Director's office.

The rain and wind were still as strong as they'd been at the start of the monsoon. A knot of people stood outside the main door, huddled under the awning in the hope of even a brief letup. Yeong-pyo pushed past, out into the street, muttering to himself that it was all right for some.

Each step threw up a splash of muddy water, while thin streams of rain poured over his chin. His armpits began to prickle with heat, a sign that his worked-up mood had provoked his liver, which had begun to harden as it lost its battle with the disease. But Yeong-pyo rarely had the luxury of attending to his pain. His son had an "incurable sickness" of his own, and one whose remedy was far more urgent. As he walked, Yeong-pyo unconsciously tightened his grip on the bottle concealed in his trouser pocket, squeezing so hard that the plastic buckled. For the second time that day, a voice from the past echoed in his ears.

To bring your son to his senses . . .

But the voice wasn't that of the Bowibu director; instead, it belonged to the director of military security, who'd spoken those same words—*To bring your son to his senses*—almost a year ago when Kyeong-hun had been demobilized.

Strictly speaking, your son should have been packed off to political prisoners' camp, but I invented a "Fault 1 Demobilization" instead. We're colleagues, and I wanted to give you the chance to bring your son to his senses. I've enclosed his written statement with this letter; once you've read it, you'll understand that further leniency simply wouldn't have been possible, under the circumstances. This young man is more canny than he's letting on.

Yeong-pyo had raced through the letter, then unfolded his son's statement with a trembling hand.

I have been accused of a heinous crime against the Party and our Great Leader, General Kim Il-sung. My comrade from the security department claims that my brain has been rotted by the South Korean puppets' anti-Communist broadcasts that parrot ideas of "freedom." I acknowledge the truth of this. It was while stationed as a border sentry on the 38th parallel, where I had been assigned in order to prepare for the military arts festival, that I was subjected to this constant barrage of "freedom" propaganda. These broadcasts hounded me every hour of the day; there was nowhere to go to escape them, and nor was it feasible to go around with my hands over my ears. The crime of which I am accused was committed on Saturday evening. We had held a dress rehearsal in the presence of the director of the political department, and then received criticism for our performance.

"Today's rehearsal was extremely mediocre. I pride myself on being a man of culture, and I've attended enough plays and recitals to know what is meant by 'stage truth.' You might not be familiar with the term, but you should at least understand the concept, how actors perform a given play as though it were real life. To lie, in other words, but convincingly, so the audience will believe it is the truth. But was there anything convincing about the awkward, stilted performance I just witnessed? No, Comrades, there was not. Stage truth can be achieved only with complete mental and physical control. Has your training taught you nothing more than how to pipe a few tunes on a tin whistle?"

This was the comrade director's evaluation of our performance. As punishment, we were ordered to do practice drills, and though there was a lot of grumbling at this, because the drills are exhausting, and we were already hungry, still we set to it in earnest. At ten o'clock the comrade director returned, apparently to check that we were doing the drills properly. It just so happened that my storytelling troupe were the ones on stage, while the rest were waiting their turn in the audience seats. The director watched us for a minute or so, then told us to take a break. Seeing us throw ourselves into the drills so wholeheartedly must have appeased his anger at our shoddy acting.

"How do you find the drills?" he asked. "Tough, no?"

"It's nothing!" the troupe cried out as one. The only ones who remained sullen and silent were myself and Comrade Oh Hak-nam, whose father is a jidowon in one of the provinces.

"You must be hungry, though?"

"Not at all!" came the answer. As if that wasn't enough, Comrade Kang Gil-nam felt the need to yell out, "We aren't gluttons obsessed with filling our bellies!" and the rest of the troupe then bellowed their assent, drumming their heels. I was genuinely taken aback. This was the same Kang Gil-nam who, only a few moments ago when he'd stumbled during one of the drills, had been griping about how it was no wonder we were so weak, "living off chicken feed." And not just him; back then the rest had been perfectly quick to join in, even cracking jokes about their navels being in love with their spines, as the two were clearly hankering for a kiss.

So how were they now contradicting themselves so convincingly? Might this be the "stage truth" that the comrade director had talked about? I couldn't say; unlike him, I'm no connoisseur of the arts. And wasn't it even more bizarre that only Comrade Hak-nam and I, whose fathers are both high-ranking cadres, had been unable to join in this display of acting talent, instead presenting the comrade director with expressions more suited to a constipated dog?

In any case, after briefly exhorting us to carry on, saying we'd do well to apply the same effort to our rehearsals, the director disappeared back inside, out of the cold. He'd said he would be back again at 11 p.m. to settle up, but 11:30 p.m. and then midnight both went by with no sight of him. By this point, we were too exhausted and strung out to carry on drilling.

And so we all—storytellers, singers, and accompanists— huddled around the drum stove, which was a tight squeeze for forty-odd people, and which in any case was producing more smoke than actual heat, as we had only unseasoned firewood to burn. Some tried to make the time go faster by cracking jokes, but they ended up being pretty damp squibs; we were just too cold to be properly funny. Not that this mattered; as usual in such a situation, where gut-wrenching rage had to be forcibly suppressed, we were ready to fall about laughing if anyone so much as coughed a bit strangely. It was almost like some kind of laughing sickness.

Someone hissed at us to be quiet and we all pricked up our ears, thinking he'd heard the director's footsteps; then a drawn-out fart ripped through the silence and we all roared our heads off. Though I laughed with the rest of them, in spite or perhaps because of our sorry situation, I could feel something boiling inside me. First, I couldn't help suspecting that we wouldn't have been abandoned for so long if it hadn't been for foolish bravado. My feelings toward those comrades of mine who'd pretended to be immune to hunger and fatigue weren't exactly benevolent. On top of that, it really was bitterly cold.

But worst of all was that I'd been assigned a skit called "The Bottomless Mess Tin," meaning I'd had to spend half the night pretending to be devouring all manner of delicious things while in reality my stomach was as cold and hollow as an empty cellar. It really stuck in my craw, I can tell you. I whipped out a cigarette in a fit of pique, but no sooner had I stuck it between my lips than the drill leader decided we'd sat around for long enough and ordered us to "resume, starting with the comedy skit."

Why that damned skit first, of all things? I thought, and before I realized what I was doing I was on my feet. "Never mind the skit," I shouted, bounding up onto the stage, "I'll improvise something that'll have you in awe of my stage truth." This was what had been building up inside me, straining to get out, and there was just no way to hold it in any longer. "Hmm, what shall I do about a title? I've got it! 'It Hurts, Hahaha,' to be followed by a second act called 'It Tickles, Boohoo!'"

While the others laughed at my antics, I slipped behind the stage curtains before turning around and poking my head out, making sure that only my face was visible. Even now, I can't understand how something I'd dreamed up on the spot managed to flow so seamlessly. "Ladies and gentlemen!" I cried. "At this very moment, behind the curtains where you cannot see, I'm being pricked with a whole host of needles. But the director commands me to laugh! Go on, one of you lot be the director."

"Laugh!" someone shouted obediently, and I instantly responded by contorting my face into a grotesquely exaggerated mask of pain, stretching my mouth as wide as it would go before parodying, to the best of my ability, the spectacle of sobs gradually transforming into laughter, crying first "Boohoo" and then "Haha." The others were in stitches. They were still wiping away the tears when I popped out from behind the curtains and announced the second act. But I was interrupted by Kang Gil-nam, leaping up to join me on stage.

"I'll do Act Two!" he announced, darting behind the curtains and poking his face out just as I had.

"You, Comrade? Very well! Right, so this time . . . Got it! Ladies and gentlemen, allow me to introduce Comrade Kang, a budding actor in his twenty-third year of drama school."

"Nonsense, how can anyone be a student for twenty-three years?" a female comrade called out.

"Ah well, if you don't know, I can't tell you! This second act, as previously announced, is a piece by the name of 'It Tickles, Boohoo.' Right! A soft set of fingers begin to inch their way up to Comrade Kang's armpit . . . one step . . . two steps . . ."

"Hahahahaha! Uh-uh . . . boohoo." As an actor, Comrade Kang was head and shoulders above me. The others were clutching their ribs and begging him to stop.

They say laughter is the best tonic, and the others did indeed appear all the better for our comic interlude. Once they were sufficiently recovered, it was back to the drills, and this time there were no complaints.

This account is a full and detailed explanation of my crime, a crime for which I humbly beg forgiveness. The broadcasts of the bastard South Koreans must genuinely have rotted my mind.

As to why I chose those particular titles for my improvised performances, something which the comrade director has asked me to clarify, surely it is not such an uncommon idea, having to laugh at something to stop yourself from crying, and vice versa?

Those were just the first titles that popped into my head, seeing how Comrade Kang and the others refused to admit to their hunger, and thinking of myself having to perform "The Bottomless Mess Tin" while my stomach felt as though it might devour itself.

Second, as to why I described Kang Gil-nam as a twenty-third-year drama student, again, it was the first thing that popped into my head, as Comrade Kang is twenty-three years old. This is the honest truth. I never would have dreamed that this foolish clowning of mine would be a matter for the security department. Again, I can only beg forgiveness.

"You louse!" The same exclamation that Yeong-pyo had spat out on first reading that statement now sprang once more from his mouth, awash with the taste of rainwater. It stood to reason that as the son of someone high up in the Bowibu, Kyeong-hun had had a sheltered adolescence, but how, at his age, could he still not have grasped the workings of the world in which he lived?

A year ago, Yeong-pyo had been willing to turn a blind eye to the incident of the comic skit, but for the same misdeeds to be repeated today was too much. Any action, any utterance, was observed and documented, not only in the military theater or the foothills of Mount Baekryeon, but even a thousand *ri* underground—was it conceivable that Kyeong-hun could be ignorant of this? Could he really be so idiotic? No. Just as the military director had written, though Kyeong-hun had clearly intended his written statement to come across as the account of a naïve, wide-eyed young man, in reality he was "more canny than he's letting on."

That louse of a son has his head on backward, and it's those damned liberalization broadcasts that have spun it around for him—180 degrees, until he can't tell north from south. Would there be the slightest blemish on his record otherwise, would he even cast his eyes at this Kim Suk-i? Kim Suk-i, who everyone knows is the daughter of a political prisoner!

Recalling all the trouble he'd had extracting a promise from Kyeong-hun to break off the relationship—like getting blood out of a stone—Yeong-pyo swore under his breath and dashed the rainwater off his chin. To his surprise, he found himself already home; he'd been too preoccupied to notice his surroundings.

"Is Kyeong-hun here?" he snapped, only halfway across the threshold.

"Not yet, and with this rain . . ." Unable to gauge her husband's mood, Kim Sun-shil had no way of knowing her words would only provoke him further. "I'm getting quite worried, you know."

"Hah! Don't waste your time."

"What? How can I not worry? Only today, two people from the food factory were killed in a landslide while picking flowers in the mountains, and the little boy who got bitten by a snake yesterday died this morning."

"Yes, yes, all right."

Nothing irritated Yeong-pyo so much as having to listen to someone tell him what he already knew. Though it was less than a week since the official mourning period for Kim Il-sung had begun, anything that passed for a flower bed had already

163

been stripped bare. It was impossible to find even a single bloom in the small gardens attached to residential blocks, let alone in the public streets and parks.

Though this hadn't been made public, a day or two into the mourning period people had cottoned on to the fact that their visits to lay flowers at one of the newly erected altars were being secretly tallied. Not only had one such visit per day become a hard-and-fast law, but there were even people who went once before each mealtime, morning, noon, and night. There were hundreds of altars all across the city, in local Party offices, factories, even schools, and what with each of the five-hundred-thousand-odd inhabitants requiring a steady supply of flowers to take there, there was nothing for it but to send workers and pupils out of the city to gather wildflowers. In Yeong-pyo's unit, the daily task of picking enough flowers for each member to lay a bouquet at the altar was delegated on rotation.

Children and adults alike roamed the mountains, and with the monsoon season making the ground treacherous, frequent accidents were only to be expected. Yeong-pyo's wife's anxiety was far from baseless. But this wasn't enough to smooth the edges of his temper.

"If that damned louse dies in the mountains, good riddance!"

"What?"

"Look at this." Yeong-pyo tugged the bottle out of the pocket of his sodden trousers and threw it onto the floor.

"What's that?"

"What does it look like? Alcohol!" Yeong-pyo took himself off into the next room, sliding the door roughly closed behind him.

Kim Sun-shil narrowed her eyes in annoyance, frustrated by the conversation's having been cut short before it had properly got going. That husband of hers, so conservative and uptight that even today, after their more than three decades as man and wife, he would only ever get changed behind closed doors!

"Well, what about it?" she called through, her curiosity tinged with alarm. "What's it got to do with us?"

"Don't you know a piece of evidence when you see it? Evidence of debauchery, lasciviousness, self-indulgence . . ." Yeong-pyo interrupted himself with a groan; he was clearly having difficulty removing his wet clothes. "He was supposed to be picking flowers, but it was a different young bud he was after."

"Kyeong-hun, you mean? And who was the 'young bud'?"

"Kim Suk-i."

"What?!" Sun-shil swept the door open, causing her husband to hastily yank his trousers up. He needn't have bothered; his wife's vision was entirely filled by the faces of the two Suk-is, who were known at the factory as Big and Little. "Which Kim Suk-i? That Big Suk-i again?"

"Would I be here now if I was sure of that? I would have gone to hunt down that louse of a son and put a bullet in his head!" Yeong-pyo gripped the belt of his trousers near the holster and shook it so violently he threatened to do himself an injury. His matchstick waist sticking out above the belt looked narrow enough to have fitted down a single trouser leg. "In fact, we've had a stroke of luck. Whoever the agents were, they were too dim-witted to do a thorough job of it. Their report didn't clarify which Suk-i it was."

"It must have been that Big Suk-i. He must have started up with her again."

"What makes you so sure?"

"I'm guessing, of course. I know you did everything to separate them."

Biting her fingernails in a nervous reflex, Sun-shil let her gaze stray to the sunflower outside the window.

Somehow those resplendent petals had managed to keep their shape even while being battered by the rains, and perhaps it had something to do with this impressive appearance, as well as the plant's towering height, that led them to be overlaid in Sun-shil's mind's eye with a dazzling face. It belonged, of course, to her son Kyeong-hun, a strapping lad whose wavy hair undulated like grass in the wind. His broad, open forehead gave him an air of intelligence, while his slightly upturned eyes denoted keen perception. In other words, he had a face that seemed well suited to being buried in a book, as Kyeong-hun's so frequently was.

At some point early on in their marriage, her husband had made what she'd assumed at the time was a joke, though this was out of keeping with his serious, somewhat po-faced character: *I've always been regarded as a stickler, my heart as gnarled and knotty as an old tree, and I'm determined not to pass such qualities on to my offspring. That's why I made such heroic efforts to win your hand—I wanted your height, your fine features, your artistic talent. And so, if I'm to see my wish come true, you must bear me a son who takes after you. . . .*

And Yeong-pyo's wish had indeed come true, though in this case he would have been wise to heed the old adage "Be careful what you wish for." After all the effort he'd made to rid himself of those ugly traits, he now had his own son to thank for a whole new set of pains. When it came to personal conduct and an understanding of the ways of the world, Kyeong-hun would be found sorely lacking if measured against his father.

It hadn't been that long ago that Yeong-pyo had forced Kyeong-hun to promise to break off with Big Suk-i. Sun-shil had been giving the house its evening tidying when she noticed something out of place—an official document lying casually unfolded between the neat stacks of filed papers on her husband's desk. No sooner had she scanned the heading, "Order for the Deportation of the Family of Kim Sung-bin," than her puzzled frown transformed into a look of horror. Wide-eyed, she skimmed down to read that, for various reasons, the wife and children of Kim Sung-bin were to join him in a labor camp for political prisoners. There was only one Kim Sung-bin she knew of to whom such an order might apply—Big Suk-i's father. Sun-shil swiftly tucked the paper into her jacket pocket, glancing around nervously as though she might have been being watched. She hurried off in search of her husband, and thrust the document in front of him with a trembling hand.

"Even monkeys occasionally fall from trees, they say, but how could you be so careless? To bring such a thing into our house, and then to leave it lying around for anyone to see!"

"There are times the monkey falls, but there are also times it only pretends to."

"But is it true? Is the family going to be deported?"

"Damn it, what did I just say about pretending? Put that back where you found it!"

Only then did Sun-shil realize that this was all a ruse of her husband's, deliberately designed to gauge the level of Kyeong-hun's affection for Kim Suk-i—and ideally to disperse it.

Sure enough, Kyeong-hun rose to the bait. A few days later, the three of them had settled down in front of the TV for an after-dinner film, *Outpost Line*. Not long in, Kyeong-hun was heard to mutter something, apparently in response to the action on-screen. His words were muffled, as though spoken to himself, but Yeong-pyo's sharp ears pricked up.

"It's the same now as it was back then—class enemies are still cut from the same cloth."

"So you do have some sense, after all!" Yeong-pyo exclaimed.

"Haha, father, do you really think I'm such a lost cause? It's just that, you know, I tend to apply our Party's policy of 'benevolence and tolerance' when I look at others."

"Such a policy is all well and good, but it can't just be applied indiscriminately; leniency is intended only for those who merit it." Yeong-pyo's reproof was mild, his tone sympathetic;

such a harmonious conversation between father and son was almost unprecedented.

"Indeed," Kyeong-hun responded, "and if the Bowibu is to be as effective as possible I think you have to be ruthless in determining who merits the opposite. A bad apple rots the barrel, isn't that what they say? It's not enough to crack down on a single individual; the entire family ought to be purged. Families, for example, like—well, it's a little awkward for me to say this, given the relationship I was recently involved in, but like that of Big Kim Suk-i."

"Now, now," Yeong-pyo blustered, "whatever are you—"

"Don't you think I have eyes in my head, Father?"

"Ach, how could I have been so careless? That document I left on my desk . . ."

In this way, the two men's verbal fencing seemed to have ended with the elder on top. As far as Yeong-pyo could see, Kyeong-hun had as much as renounced any connection with Big Suk-i. Only Sun-shil was unconvinced by this apparent triumph. Her husband might have prided himself on his cunning in catching a slippery fish, but to her the fish seemed strangely eager to take the bait, even casting itself up onto dry land without waiting to be reeled in.

Now, judging by recent developments, it was clear that Yeong-pyo had been the one taken in that day—hook, line, and sinker. No matter how much Sun-shil wanted to believe otherwise, there wasn't a scrap of evidence that might suggest it was the other Suk-i that Kyeong-hun had gotten mixed up with. Why, the pair had never been known to exchange even a casual remark! And yet, even while perfectly aware of this, Sun-shil and Yeong-pyo could not quite bring themselves to relinquish the possibility that it was indeed Little Suk-i. But they knew they were deluding themselves. If nothing else, Kyeong-hun simply wasn't the type to cast a young woman aside like a bit of old rubbish because his parents were opposed to the match.

Sun-shil's chest felt suddenly tight. This time, the scene that swam hazily into her head was that of her husband and Kyeong-hun's eventual clash, which had genuinely threatened to end in a gunshot.

"Hand me my umbrella!" Sun-shil started at this barked command, jerked abruptly back to the present. She turned away from the window and moved to pass her husband his umbrella.

"Where are you off to now?"

"The factory altar," Yeong-pyo snapped over his shoulder, already halfway out of the door. "The nation is in mourning, even if it that crazy bastard has forgotten it!"

Sun-shil had just finished preparing dinner when Kyeong-hun arrived home, his sopping clothes and squelching shoes making him look as though he'd been put through a wringer. He'd had to stop by each household affiliated with his factory, to distribute that day's allocation of flowers. Yeong-pyo arrived home not long afterward, having had his own rounds to make—checking in on his agents, who were stationed at every local altar.

"Dinner's ready!" Sun-shil seemed anxious to get the meal out of the way before a squall blew up, but Yeong-pyo had no time for such niceties. He looked over at Kyeong-hun, who, after changing out of his wet clothes and running a comb through his hair, had promptly installed himself on one of the floor's warm spots and buried his nose in a book. The boy was the picture of innocence, which only served to boil Yeong-pyo's already hot blood.

"Close that book." Yeong-pyo's voice was cold as ice. Kyeong-hun glanced up, tilting his head to one side and widening his eyes in an affectation of puzzled surprise. "You ought to show more care when you go to pick flowers."

"Oh, but I am careful. What with this recent spate of accidents—"

"Acting, again!"

"Why, Father, whatever do you mean?"

"I had to stand in the meeting room today and have my name dragged through the mud. And not just my name—my whole political career!"

"Really? But surely not because of me?"

"Oh, 'surely not,' is it? You worthless brat! You swan around plying yourself with alcohol in this time of national mourning, and have the gall to play the innocent!"

"There must be some misunderstanding; could you be a little clearer?"

"Clearer!" Yeong-pyo whipped the plastic bottle out from underneath the table and slammed it against the table with

171

such force it might have been driven into the wood if it had been made of a harder material. "This seems clear enough! What do you have to say for yourself?"

"I'm afraid I can't think of much. It looks like a perfectly ordinary bottle to me."

"So perfectly ordinary that you don't remember drinking out of it? And how about the girl you were drinking with? I suppose you don't remember her either? The same Kim Suk-i whose family you denounced in this very room? Have I jogged your memory yet?"

"I see. So you heard this from the Bowibu director?"

"You admit it, then!"

"That's right, it's all coming back to me now. This bottle . . . and the rest . . ." Kyeong-hun gulped, and the sound of his dry throat convulsing made his mother flinch.

"Kyeong-hun!" Sun-shil broke in, hoping to defuse the situation while there was still time. "If you were any other worker who'd stepped out of line, your father would simply punish you and have done with it. You know that, don't you? It's for your own good that he's trying to make you see reason. Isn't it time you put your shameful discharge from the army behind you and started making something of your life?"

"I understand, Mother, honestly I do. But can't a man hold his female comrade's hand when they're walking along the edge of a cliff? A comrade whom he works with every day?"

"It was Big Suk-i, then?" Yeong-pyo's lip curled in disgust.

"Yes."

"So it was all an act, that spiel you came out with while we were watching *Outpost Line*?" Yeong-pyo ground the words out from between clenched teeth.

"I'm sorry. That was . . . Forgive me. But I wasn't the only one acting, was I, Father? You were the one who began it, pretending to have accidentally left a classified document lying around in plain view. You, who've never made the slightest misstep in your whole career! How was I supposed to respond? I went along with the performance only because I wanted to reassure you, both of you. I didn't want you worrying about Big Suk-i."

"What is there between you two?"

"Well, I can't see myself marrying her, so you can rest easy on that count. But I can't just cast her aside, either. She's someone for whom I feel a deep affection—proper comradely affection, you understand, all aboveboard—and a great deal of sympathy, too. She has so many talents, yet she'll never be given the chance to shine. And after all, what was her father's great crime? Only to say that Kim Jong-il had taken a second wife, which everyone knows is true."

"Quiet!" The plastic bottle flew through the air and struck Kyeong-hun's cheek. "You're a dyed-in-the-wool reactionary! No wonder you get drunk when you should be shedding tears."

For Kyeong-hun, this appeared to be the final straw. His hand had flown up to his stinging cheek; now it trembled as he held it there, almost imperceptibly mirroring his twitching lips, which he pressed even more firmly together as though battling to hold his emotions inside. Suffering under an equal strain, Sun-shil held her breath and wrung her hands as her gaze flicked nervously between the two men.

After a brief while, Kyeong-hun recovered himself sufficiently to be able to open his mouth and speak in a relatively measured tone, though one which hummed with an undercurrent of agitation.

"Father, this is too much! I might not be winning any medals for loyalty, but I know the proper conduct for mourning the deceased. Have you ever heard of someone drinking meths?"

"What?"

"Soaking your clothes in methyl spirits is proven to ward off snakes; that's what was in that bottle I had with me. If you don't believe me, you can call Mr. Park at the lab right now. He's the one I borrowed it from."

"Kyeong-hun!" Choking out her son's name, Sun-shil pressed his hands between her own. Tears spilled like a shower of rain from her eyes, still bright despite the lines of age.

Witnessing his mother's distress caused Kyeong-hun's eyes to tear up in response. All that his "twenty-six years of drama school" had taught him to bury deep inside him now refused to be suppressed any longer

"Don't you see how miserable it all is? How wretched? People who are so eager to catch others out, they'll even scrabble around after rubbish like this." He gestured angrily toward the bottle at his feet. "A sincere, genuine life is possible only for those who have freedom. Where emotions are suppressed and actions monitored, acting only becomes ubiquitous, and so convincing that we even trick ourselves. Look at all these people, sobbing over a death that happened three months ago, starving because they haven't been able to draw their rations all the while. What about the mother of the child bitten by a snake while he was out gathering flowers for Kim Il-sung's altar? Perhaps she finds her private grief useful for shedding public tears. Isn't it frightening, this society which teaches us all to be great actors, able to turn on the waterworks at the drop of a hat?"

"Shut up, you little idiot! Enough of this reactionary nonsense!"

"But those who see forced tears as a sign of loyalty, of solidarity? Aren't they the real idiots? Surely you know that whatever the play, the curtain always falls in the end."

A strangled cry emerged from Yeong-pyo's throat as he flew out of his chair, fumbling at his waist as though in the grip of some violent compulsion.

"What are you doing?" Sun-shil rushed to place herself between husband and son, staring at the former with a look of horror.

"Out of my way!" With one hand, Yeong-pyo thrust his wife aside, while in the other, the metallic gleam of the gun's muzzle announced its venomous bite.

"Go ahead, shoot," Kyeong-hun said, standing up and spreading his arms to bare his chest. "Kill me, if that's truly what you want! But even if you fill this body with bullets, you'll never kill my wish to live a life fit for a human being!"

A gunshot rang out in reply, and the room was abruptly plunged into darkness. There was a brief shocked silence, broken then by Sun-shil's keening as she crawled on her knees to where she guessed her son had been standing. Flailing madly, she bumped her shoulder against the table, and something clattered noisily to the floor. The echoes had barely died down when the telephone's harsh ring made her jump, the sound seeming strangely incongruous.

"Is it a blackout? The garage . . . Get to the garage! Send cars out to the altars and light them up! Hurry!"

Sun-shil couldn't tell whether these words were coming from this world or the next. But then she felt a hand clutch hers.

"Mother!" Here he was, her son, bawling like a baby as she felt up his arm to check his shoulder, his head. There was the sound of the front door being flung open and footsteps racing out. The night was pitch-black, the sky free of even a single point of light. Though the rain had finally let up, the wind was howling with renewed vigor. The sound of a hundred whips slamming into the air filled the space between heaven and earth.

Yeong-pyo raced headlong down the stairs and out to the factory's main gate, where an altar had been set up beneath a large oil painting of Kim Il-sung, adorned with the inscription "We will worship the Great Leader until the sun and moon go out." It had been installed by the gate, as the company common room was far too small to accommodate the thousands of employees who made a daily pilgrimage of mourning. The cars that had been driven out—on Yeong-pyo's directive—were already parked in a semicircle, arranged so

that the beams from their headlights were best placed to illuminate the altar. There were five of them, lighting up the
marble plinth so brightly that each petal on each bouquet
could be clearly picked out. A drawn-out chorus of wailing
was audible even in spite of the wind's almighty din.

A fixed complement of mourners was guaranteed at any
one time; when one left he or she would be instantly replaced,
just as the water level is regulated in an artificial lake. Seeing
the ebb and flow around the altar operating just as it should,
Yeong-pyo ought to have felt sufficiently at ease to go and sit
in one of the cars and get out of the wind. But there was no
way he could sit easy at a time like this.

He needed to get a good look at the current crop of
mourners. Was it true that they were merely actors, crying
fabricated tears? Kyeong-hun's words still rang shrill in his
ears, whipping up a storm of confusion. He pulled the brim of
his hat low over his eyes and slipped into the wailing throng.
Almost immediately his gaze landed on the mother of Big
Kim Suk-i, a painful shock to his already frayed nerves. That
she, of all people, would be standing right in front of the
altar . . . What kind of trickery was this?

When he'd had the impulse to conceal himself among
the crowd, to assess the sincerity of their grief, wasn't this
woman from Haeju precisely whom he'd had in mind, her
husband languishing in a political prisoners' camp, always
complaining that her family was on the brink of starvation?
Now, faced with the sight of the real-life woman laying her
bouquet on the altar with a heart-rending cry of "Great Leader,

Father!" Yeong-pyo trembled. The tears were streaming down her cheeks! It was shocking, appalling, something that Yeong-pyo would never have considered possible even if he'd read it in one of his agent's reports. He felt as though he had stumbled into the presence of a nine-tailed fox, a cunning, treacherous creature who must be avoided at all costs.

Turning and stumbling back, Yeong-pyo was in too much haste to extricate himself from the crowd of mourners to worry about drawing attention to himself. Pain was radiating from his liver, yet he could not have been said to feel it. A shrill whine throbbed in both his ears, as though a flock of cicadas was trapped inside his skull. What he had just witnessed felt as unreal as a dream. Such tears were not to be believed.

If even someone like Big Suk-i's mother was able to sob convincingly, to cry out "Great Leader!" in a suitably mournful tone . . . But how were they managing to squeeze out actual tears? Did they carry bottles of water concealed about their person, to splash on their faces when no one was looking?

It's called stage truth.

Who said that? The voice had sounded like Kyeong-hun's, but also like that of an old army comrade of his. . . .

Stage truth . . . As Yeong-pyo dragged himself over to a corner, his feet seemed to move of their own accord, while his mind, unmoored, drifted further from the here and now. *That's right. Anyone who has that can produce a few tears, even Big Suk-i's mother. But it usually takes an experienced actor to really pull it off. . . .*

178

After all this time, have you still not figured out that that's exactly what she is? That voice again—who was it? Could it be that Kang Gil-nam, who had insisted on performing the second improvisation? *A woman like her, with forty-five years of acting school under her belt, forty-five years in which to master the only scenarios she'll ever need: "It Hurts, Haha"; "It Tickles, Boohoo." And no wonder she's excelled, with you to train her up. Strict teachers are always the most effective.*

Forty-five years? But she can't be older than forty-five now. And I'm the one who trained her, who taught her the cunning of a nine-tailed fox? Me?

Yes, you, Father. You've had fifty-eight years of the same training, after all, and you've always been top of your class.

Kyeong-hun, you bastard! I ought to have put a bullet in you just now. I don't know where you got it from, this insolence, this insubordination . . . but it has nothing to do with me. Nothing, do you hear me?

You're too modest, father. You gave a display of your talent only this morning; how to produce a pitcher's worth of tears from a cup of sadness.

What are you talking about, "this morning"?

In front of the Bowibu director. And it came in handy, didn't it?

What? I, I don't know what you're talking about. I don't know. I don't . . .

Yeong-pyo caught his foot on something, stumbled, and fell. Groaning, he struggled to his feet, but seemed to have left his disordered mind scattered over the ground. He stood, his features blank and uncomprehending. The gusting wind tugged at his clothes.

"Eoi, eoi!"

That sound, threaded through the howl of the wind like the keening cry of some water sprite, making the hairs stand up on the back of his neck— could such a mournful wail really have come from Big Suk-i's mother? Was it possible?

Yeong-pyo trembled all over. He had blundered over to the small park, off to one side of the deserted factory buildings. But his immediate surroundings had passed beyond his comprehension. The altar's brilliant halo filled a vacant gaze, in which the pupils had come unmoored. The intersecting beams from the cars' headlights resembled theater spotlights. One beam stretched all the way to where Yeong-pyo was standing, illuminating the somber pines and low stone benches.

"These pines are wonderfully drawn—just like the real thing! Wait a minute, whose scene is this? Ah, that's right, that's right. . . ."

Passing between the trees, a trainer took the stage. A trainer bearing the indelible stain of a horrifying crime, who must now press the barrel of a gun to his temple and bring this whole matter to a close.

The bang of the gun ripped through the warm night air, but Yeong-pyo was beyond hearing it. Hong Yeong-pyo, a stern director who had demanded the same stage truth no less from himself than from others, had chosen to bring the curtain down, in advance of that of his fellow actors.

29th January, 1995

The Red Mushroom

There was a very simple reason that the inhabitants of N Town referred to the municipal government office as "the redbrick house"—its bricks were conspicuously red. Indeed, the government office stood out among the street's other brick buildings as conspicuously red. It had gone up in the early days after liberation, when the Communist Party was only recently established, and a Party secretary at the time had instructed that specially made bricks be used, into which some kind of red coloring had been mixed.

The secretary in question, a lion-headed man who had the words of Marx's *Communist Manifesto* constantly on his lips and a tobacco pipe always in hand, had declared that the building must be red outside as well as in, as it had sprouted from seeds sown by that red specter from Europe. He had the red coloring added not only to the bricks but also to the roof tiles, making the Communist Party office truly a red house. Once you took all this into consideration, the innocuous phrase "the redbrick house" necessarily denoted not some ordinary building, but the color red—startling, conspicuous, almost extravagant.

So if some snotty-nosed kid said to another, "Think you can do what you like 'cause you're a redbrick-house kid?" that of course meant that the one being addressed was the child of someone who worked at the Party office. And if a woman said, with a roll of her eyes, "Forget it—she's a redbrick-house wife," one of two things was certain: Either the woman in question worked at the red house, or her husband did.

Hoe Yunmo, a reporter for the district's daily newspaper, was sitting at his desk when a gust of wind swept in through the window, whisked his notepad up from in front of him, and tossed it onto the floor. Only this succeeded in shaking him out of his paralysis.

"Damn it!" he grumbled, bending to pick up the pad. But it wasn't the breeze he was cursing. He'd been told to write an article, yet hadn't managed to produce so much as a single line; his own wandering thoughts were the cause of his annoyance, as he loitered in the vicinity of the brick house instead of concentrating on the task at hand. Why now of all times, when he should have been acting as though he'd had a fire lit under him, was his mind insisting on dredging up the origins and circumstances of that building, something which could not have been further from his subject? On his pad, which he had now set back on the desk, there was still nothing other than a title: "N Town's Bean Paste Factory Returns to Normal Production Levels."

Yunmo flung his fountain pen down onto the notepad and rubbed his face with his hands. His dry mouth produced a croak of dismay quite of its own accord. Over a decade on the job, and he could have sworn he'd never had writer's block this bad.

It was like a skewer being inserted into his brain: He simply could not ignore the thought that even in cases when the order came from the redbrick house and should therefore be obeyed without hesitation, there were some instances in which it was simply not possible to produce what was required—as impossible as making yourself cry on command. It had been close to three months since the town's production of soybean paste had slumped from sporadic to nonexistent, yet Yunmo was now expected to write an article on the factory's return to normal operation—like reporting on the news of a birth before conception had even occurred!

Three days previously, when the lion-headed secretary in charge of the redbrick house had called him up and requested the article, Yunmo had been struck dumb. He could picture the secretary's childish moon face, which bore an unvarying look of contempt regardless of whom he was addressing.

"What, no comment? Hahaha. Why, there's as much coming out of your mouth as there is from the factory's soybean tank. . . ."

This sly joke was made in a voice whose high pitch was all the more conspicuous for having emerged from a veritable tree trunk of a neck, sandwiched between face and shoulders of equal corpulence. "Our town has been receiving a lot of criticism over this issue. Which is, of course, entirely the fault of the irresponsible behavior of certain workers. But now that the factory's bean paste tank is going to open its mouth and give us all we want, you reporters need to start doing the same. 'Yes, I *will* write the article,' that kind of thing. Ha!" As soon as it seemed the joke had finished, the secretary let his laughter fade away and resumed his customary tone of contempt. "The article should come out before the end of the month. Got it?"

That day, Yunmo dutifully set out on the road which the secretary had laid in front of him and visited the bean paste factory. The manager who greeted him there was so gaunt he looked like a stick of wood in clothes; even his bald head gave the impression of being somehow hollow.

"Yes, yes. It's all true. We're back at the fermentation stage now. What are we fermenting? Thanks to the support of the local Party, we've been provided with acorns and corn from the farms, thirty tons in all. That will give us enough for a month's supply of bean paste."

Not a year's supply—a month's. So this was the situation as it really stood: To people who had by now already forgotten the taste of bean paste and who might not even set eyes on such a thing for a long time, Yunmo was expected to trumpet the lie that the factory had returned to normal production levels. Though this would hardly be the first time he'd been creative with the truth. A fair few of the newspaper's readers had their own name for Yunmo—Mr. Bullshit Reporter. And even he had to admit that this wasn't exactly groundless.

Yunmo unscrewed the lid of his thermos and tilted the bottle to his lips. It was alcohol. For him, alcohol was the lubricant he needed to produce the bullshit articles he was assigned, a bad habit so long ingrained that he now couldn't remember a time without it.

"Yunmo, are you there?"

Someone was banging on the door. Before Yunmo even had time to screw the lid of the thermos back on, Song, a consulting doctor at the hospital, burst into the room. The two were friends from childhood, having grown up hopping about on sugarcane stilts together and been lab partners in middle school. They may have been opposites physically—Yunmo was tall and heavyset with somewhat coarse features, while everything about Song was small and neat—the two men were still as close as they'd ever been, and frequently confided in each other.

"What's the matter?"

Shocked by the sight of Song's pale, sweating face, Yunmo got quickly up from his seat.

"Yunmo, you have to help me. My uncle's just been arrested."

"What? You mean the one who's an engineer at the bean paste factory?"

"Apparently they came for him while he was working out in the fields, all covered in dust. What are we going to do?"

"Go back to the beginning and explain it for me, step by step. Why has this happened?"

"Dereliction of duty—that's what they're calling it; that's what they're branding my uncle with. You wrote that article about him, you know him pretty well, no? Please help, in any way you can."

The shock looked to have shaken Song quite out of his senses. The white froth flecking his lips, his shuddering legs, painted all too clear a picture of just how serious this business was. Yunmo hastily fetched a bowl of cold water from the kitchen.

"There, drink this, sit down, and let's talk."

Yunmo got out his cigarettes and lighter. All the while, he found himself unable to shake the image of Ko Inshik, chief technician at the soybean mill, a man of weak constitution, whose eyes, behind his thick-lensed glasses, had always seemed somewhat swollen.

2

It was three years ago, at almost exactly the same week of August it was now, that Yunmo had first come to hear of Ko Inshik. On that day too, Song had come to call on Yunmo, on Inshik's behalf. The man he called his uncle was in fact only a distant cousin, but their relationship was far closer than the family tree might have suggested.

During his time attending medical college in Pyongyang, it was Inshik who had ensured that Song was able to give his studies his undivided attention, free from the loneliness often felt by the sons of widows, and also from the straitened circumstances of dormitory life. Whenever there was to be some kind of college outing, Inshik would be sure to prepare a packed lunch for him. Wordlessly, he would pass the string bag to his wife, his eyes crinkled in a smile behind his thick glasses.

That smile was what passed for conversation with him; rarely did he find himself moved to speak. That was the kind of person he was: a man of few words, but possessed of a seemingly bottomless supply of warm human kindness. Not that his wife was unsympathetic when it came to her nephew's situation, but she wouldn't have invited Song to live with them if it hadn't been for her husband's insistence. But of course, Inshik's own condition back then had been very different from what it was now.

At college, he had majored in food crop engineering, and was then appointed to a committee for light industry, tasked with overseeing technical service. In other words, he and his family were what you might call comfortably off. Many in a similar situation might have balked at sharing their wealth with others, but not Ko Inshik. When it came to kindness, he wasn't someone who knew how to do things by half measures, and it was with the deep affection of a real father that he cared for and supported Song, every day for the entire duration of his studies. And when Song graduated, neither could have guessed that in under three years' time they would find themselves both together in N Town!

When it came to light that Inshik's brother-in-law, previously assumed to have been killed by a bomb during the turmoil of the Korean War, had in fact crossed over to the South, Inshik became tarred with brush of those who "falsified their history," and was sent down from Pyongyang in order to "have the proper revolutionary ideals instilled in him" in N Town.

With this inauspicious beginning, Inshik's life in this place led Song to ponder the truth of the saying "The greater your heart, the greater your sorrows." Inshik's preeminent ability in his field of food crop engineering had secured him the position of chief technician at the bean paste factory, which would otherwise have been judged too good for him, but in all other respects his life was a thorny path.

Song had closed his aunt's eyes for the last time while her head was lying in his own lap. She, whose lips had shrunk to a colorless line, breathed her last less than two years after the trauma of being sent down from Pyongyang, with the doctors having failed to find any medical cause.

"You've ended up in this sorry state because of my brother, I know," she said to Inshik, "but I beg you, work as hard as you can so you can get back your former position."

Unable to tear her guilt-ridden gaze from her husband, and clutching the wrists of her children, she never spoke another word.

The head of any household that lacks a housewife is undoubtedly in a sorry state, as are any children who find themselves left motherless. It stood to reason that the couple's young daughter had it hard, forced to run a household and look after her younger siblings as soon as she graduated from middle school, alongside working with her father in the bean paste factory's lab. But the toll it took on Inshik was even greater, for his work supervising factory technology was burdened with an additional responsibility, on Party orders: clearing an area of land for cultivation.

For the first time in his life, Inshik was forced to try his hand at laundering a work uniform and darning socks while sitting on the threshold of a mountain hut. But it wasn't as though this preparation of the land for cultivation was devoid of perks; if that were the case, only those saddled with the taint of crime would be willing to live alone in a rough hut on a hostile, uninhabited mountain. No, there were advantages: four hundred *pyeong* of land for his own personal use, on the condition that the time and effort taken to farm it would not detract from his main tasks.

"Of course, additional perks can also be made available for those in a position of responsibility." That is what the town's chief Party secretary had told Inshik back then while notifying him of his new duties. "But bear in mind that the nature of these perks depends very much on how you acquit yourself in this task."

A weighty hint, then, that Inshik might be set free from the post of the factory's chief technician with which he had been so magnanimously entrusted—that he might even be restored to his former position. But in fact, even without this heavy hint, Inshik already had a hunch as to what the terms of the deal might be.

Simply by sending him to work in the mountains, an assignment which any laborer in the town would have balked at, the Party secretary had made it perfectly clear that they were expecting him to respond like the cow who, having secretly been eating its master's soybean leaves, flinches whenever the master moves his hand toward the whip. Whether or not it was as a direct effect of this knowledge, Inshik threw himself into his new work without hesitation. Now and then he came down to the factory to oversee the technical work there, and Song always took these opportunities to encourage him not to neglect his health, to think of his children now that their mother was gone. But Inshik would say that it was precisely the thought of his children's prospects that was spurring him on now, and go straight back to the mountains.

Three years of toil produced a large area of land reclaimed for cultivation, with soil that was ready to be planted and tilled. At the same time, Inshik's tireless improvements at the factory had also paid off, and N Town was now blessed with a glut of bean paste. "Even bean paste from Pyongyang has nothing on ours" were the words on people's lips. But they were ignorant of the secret ingredient, the salt that produced that admirable flavor—Inshik's sweat and blood.

That day three years ago, when Song sought out Yunmo and told him the story of this man Ko Inshik, he had been frank about his intentions.

"Please, if you can, write some kind of article on him, and publish it in your paper. Anything to give him a bit of a boost."

The picture which Song had painted of Inshik certainly roused Yunmo's professional ambition. Boasts about the quality of the town's bean paste had already been making him wonder whether there mightn't be a story to be had.

He decided to do some background research, the first step of which would be to visit Inshik's family. In his fairly lengthy career as a reporter, there had been many instances which cemented the truth that the best way to get an idea of people's true character is through their home life rather than their workplace.

In this case, Yunmo's experience turned out to be the best judge. Through his so-called domestic research he came to see Inshik anew, as a man whose true self had been gradually buried in his work, all undertaken in the hope of favorable treatment in the future. Yunmo chose a lunch hour to call at Inshik's house, judging that this was when someone was most likely to be home. Situated on the hill to the rear of the factory, the house was surrounded by a rather wonky fence, and a plastic tarpaulin weighted down with stones was all the storehouse had for a roof.

Even at first glance, it was clear that the place was being neglected. A boy in school uniform, who looked to be around fourteen years old, was amusing himself by hanging from the small gate which led into the front yard. Upon closer inspection, though, Yunmo saw that the boy was not playing but struggling bravely to detach a rusty chain from the gate's upper hinge. Just as Yunmo was thinking that this must be

Hye-myong, Inshik's last-born and only son, the boy pre-empted his question by announcing, "Father's not at home." Wanting to put off having to state his business, Yunmo raised his eyebrows in mock surprise, pretending not to know that Inshik was up in the mountains.

"Well, what about your sister, then?"

"She always makes up a lunch to take to work. And I take mine to school."

"So how come you're home now?" The boy seemed to quiver. "What, cat got your tongue?"

"Because . . . my sister cut her hand trying to fix this. She was crying when she went to the factory. This morning."

"Indeed! So you've come home to try to fix it before she gets back this evening. In your school lunch break, am I right?"

The boy gave no answer, only lowered his head and blinked back tears. He'd had such a battle with the chain that the sweat which slicked his small, soft hands was dyed red with rust. Yunmo felt himself pierced to the core. Seeing that the boy was on the verge of tears, he deliberately adopted a brisk, cheerful tone.

"Right, let's see what we've got here. This bastard hinge been giving you a tough time, eh? Hand me that hammer." He inserted the sharp, pronged end of the hammer between the hinge and jamb of the gate and pumped down on the handle several times, causing the gate to shriek and groan in protest. To keep the boy distracted, he punctuated these actions with some seemingly innocuous questions.

"So how come you kids are in charge of this house, as if you hadn't got a father?" The hinge popped all the way out. "Ya!"

Seeing the hinge that had obstinately refused to give in now plucked out as smoothly as a thorn by a tweezer, the boy instantly brightened.

"Father doesn't have time for anything except the cultivation site."

"Oh? What kind of work does he do there?"

"The other day when there was a parents' meeting, he just sent a note to the teacher instead. That's all we get from him as well. Even yesterday."

"I see, and what's yesterday's note about?"

"Our mother's memorial rites." As soon as those words were out of his mouth, the boy pressed his lips together, but it was too late to try to hold back his tears. Feeling extremely ill at ease, Yunmo renewed his efforts.

"There now, hold this for me. We need to get this other hinge out too. . . . Ah, this one's a real bastard!"

He began cursing and exclaiming even more vigorously than before. And it wasn't only the boy he was hoping to cheer—he could feel his own eyes on the point of tearing up. Luckily, something unexpected happened just then to put a smile on Hye-myong's face.

The hinge that Yunmo had been straining at, thinking it would prove as tough as the first one, had abruptly popped free, causing him to lose his balance and land with a thump on his backside. Though the tears still glistened in his eyes, the boy burst out laughing at the sight.

"So, Mr. Reporter, is there really a wild boar wreaking havoc in the cultivation site?"

Yunmo was startled. "How do you know I'm a reporter?"

"Ha—I knew all along. You've come to see my father."

"Why, you little rascal! But how did you find out?"

"Don't you remember? You came to our school at the start of the term and took a photo for the paper."

"Ah, so I did. But what's this all this about a wild boar?"

"Well, in his note father said it was because of some trouble with a wild boar that he couldn't come home for Mother's memorial rites."

"Oh, that must be true. Boars are a major nuisance, you know. They always go around in gangs, so even in a large cornfield they could do considerable damage in the space of a single night."

"Ah! Then it *was* true!"

"If it were me I'd miss the pair of you so much I'd want to be here all the time, but I guess things are different with your father?"

"He's busy with work . . . but he's a really good father to us. He misses us and he knows we miss him, and he really wishes he could be here for Mother's memorial rites, but he has to stay in the mountains. Every morning when he goes to wash his face at the spring, he sees our faces in the water. He wrote that in one of his letters."

"And?" Yunmo couldn't keep a tremor from his voice.

"And he gave the man who brought that letter some raspberries and mushrooms for us, and my sister used them all for mother's offertory table."

Yunmo had to avert his face. Pretending to brush the sweat from his forehead, he secretly wiped away his tears.

He took a good look around Inshik's house that day, in every nook and cranny, even taking the time to give the gate a new hinge. The house spoke eloquently of suffering, and of Inshik: a man who had painstakingly collected mushrooms as an offering for his late wife, a woman whose memorial ceremony he could not even attend; a man who had plunged his hands into brambles, hoping the raspberries might lighten his children's hearts, children whose faces he had to content himself with merely imagining. The crooked fence, the storehouse roof which could not keep out the rain gave clear expression to the fact that the man of the house was somewhere else, pouring his efforts into some other toil. The place even seemed to echo with his voice, alone on the mountain on the anniversary of his wife's death, outwardly engaged in chasing away wild boars, inwardly praying that she had found some happiness.

Afterward, Yunmo was confident that he could dash off an article in a single stretch, immediately if need be. He already had a stockpile of facts and figures relating to the cultivation site, from researching a separate issue. But by now he had fallen under the spell of Inshik's human qualities, and a burning desire grew up in him to talk face-to-face with the man himself, to be in the presence of that distinctive personality.

And so, that day, Yunmo urged himself on to the cultivation site, a distance of a hundred *ri* from the town, disregarding the scorching midday sun.

3

Rather than being stretched out in a straight line, those hundred *ri* were like a loosely folded rope. The cultivation site looked down on the town like someone peering into the depths of a well, and to get to your destination you had to double back on yourself again and again.

It was as though a sharp line had been drawn across the mountainside. The top half was still shrouded with gloomy forest, while the lower was all reclaimed land, stretching so far into the distance it was difficult to tell where it ended. This land had been divided into plots, which each held different crops—some beans, some corn, some potatoes—and its lower edge was marked by a sheer cliff, almost parallel to the tree line above. The mouth of a dark gulley gaped below.

To find a cornfield on such a steep, remote mountain was a strange and rare thing. If anything, it resembled land cleared through the ancient method known as slash-and-burn. The words "cultivation site" made it sound very modern, very technical, but if its appearance was anything to go by, then "slash-and-burn field" would have been just as appropriate.

The evidence for its having been cleared in such a way was that it was still a site filled with raw materials. Tree roots resembling dinosaur skeletons, rocks that had tumbled loose, burned stumps, all tangled up on top of one another along the furrows of the field . . . Its location so far up the mountain meant that the most innovative technology that could have been employed would have been an ox and cart. Considering that this colossal task had been achieved with a mere three bullocks and around thirty men, Yunmo looked at the stones and tree roots with fresh, wondering eyes. And it occurred to him that forty *pyeong* worth of land for personal use was a pretty poor excuse for a "perk," given the blood that had been shed in farming it.

The huts were located in the potato field, a place of relative safety.

They were low, rather scrappy-looking dwellings, constructed with unsplit logs used for rafters, which were then "papered" with bark and covered all over with soil. Yunmo approached one of these huts and stood at the entrance to the yard. The gate stood ajar, and he peered inside for a short while before setting foot inside. But just then, as though on cue, a woman's earsplitting scream burst out from inside the house.

A second scream followed in swift pursuit, that of a different woman, and Yunmo, startled, stopped in his tracks. A shriek burst from his own mouth as he saw a fat, dappled snake plop down onto his toes, squirming like a cut rope. The two maids who had just tossed it out of the kitchen, having been startled in the midst of preparing dinner for the workers, seemed even more shocked than he.

"Ah, what's this? What a time for someone to turn up!"

"Oh, and don't I know you from somewhere? The reporter? I'm so sorry. . . ."

Though the women knelt down and bowed their heads to the floor, there seemed no way to appease their feelings of guilt. Yunmo watched the snake wriggle out of the yard and into the hazelnut wood beyond. Only then did a startled laugh break from him.

"Please don't speak ill of us. This must be a first for you, Mr. Reporter, but we're all used to such things here."

"Ho, don't you worry about that. It's certainly made an impression, though. I won't go forgetting that in a hurry!"

Even as he affected a laugh, Yunmo could feel his heart-beat tripping. To steady himself, he pulled a pack of cigarettes from his trouser pocket.

"It's still hot outside; come in and sit down, quickly." The plump woman opened the door to the inner room.

"I'm all right," Yunmo said politely. "I need to speak with the comrade in charge first of all."

"Everyone goes to gather edible plants in the afternoons. This morning they were pulling the last of the weeds out of the soybean field. After all, what's the point of having salt in the kitchen if it doesn't make it into the pot? We might live on a mountain, a larder right on our doorstep, but the plants won't pick themselves."

"And even the person in charge has to pitch in?"

"Ai, who could stop him? It's in his nature to be at the front and show the way. Now, we can't have you hanging about on the threshold, so come in and sit down."

The woman's concern for his comfort was sincere, and Yunmo didn't know how to refuse. The feeling that surged up inside him as he stooped to enter the "inner room" would end up leaving just as great an impression as the snake had.

As though stepping into a Chinese house, Yunmo didn't remove his shoes before entering. The room in which he found himself was long and narrow, like the interior of a cave. A kind of mat woven from cherry bark covered the floor, and small logs of some dark wood were arranged along the back wall. Yunmo frowned, then after a pause realized that they were wooden pillows. He couldn't help being struck by the fact that the backpacks hung on both walls were clustered so tightly together the walls themselves were almost invisible. Those backpacks, clearly all each person had by way of a wardrobe or clothes chest to hold sundry essentials—in other words, the sum total of the person's "household"—were doubly striking because of their differences in color and size.

The hatch leading to the "outer room," which seemed to function as the kitchen-cum-women's quarters, was covered by a white cloth spattered with soy sauce. The strong smell of stale smoke hung in the room, mixed with that of the sweat of men.

Yunmo still didn't remove his shoes as he perched sideways on the sill of the floor, his legs tucked up to one side. Idly, he wondered which of the wooden pillows and which of the variously colored backpacks belonged to Ko Inshik. But no, surely his possessions would not be here. How could they be in such a place as this, completely open to the elements, in truth little better than some Stone Age dwelling? In the winter, the winds from Siberia would howl through this room, while in summer the air hung thick and stifling, heavy with the scent of pollen from the south.

Yunmo got up and left the room before he'd even smoked a single cigarette. The heat might be even more fierce outside, but he would still rather not be inside that house.

Not until the ball of fire that was the August sun sank behind the line of trees to the west did those who had gone out to gather plants return, trickling down from the mountain in ones and twos. Yunmo, who had been wandering here and there among the dwellings, met Ko Inshik on his return from the top of the cornfield, where the golden ears were ripening well. Inshik was carrying a gunnysack of edible mountain plants. He appeared already to be familiar with Yunmo through Song, as he held out his hand to shake as soon as the reporter had finished introducing himself. But Inshik's hand had lost the soft whiteness of the light-industries office worker he had been; nor was it the hand of a chief technician at the soybean factory. Already, that hand was as gnarled as a tree root, knuckles protruding, splotched with blood clots.

Once Inshik had let Yunmo's hand drop, he removed his thick glasses and began to polish them on the loose front of his overalls, which appeared to be a habit. In that moment, Yunmo's gaze fell on a red copper wire threaded through one of the older man's buttons, holding it in place. The wire was awfully thick; perhaps he had not been able to find anything finer.

In the future, when his thoughts would turn back to Ko Inshik, the very first thing that would spring to mind would be the copper wire that served as thread for that button.

"Let me help carry that," Yunmo said, once Inshik had put his glasses back on and shouldered his gunnysack.

"All right," Inshik conceded. Yunmo held up one corner of the sack and walked with deliberately slow steps, remarking on this and that.

Yunmo had to chatter on for some time to elicit even a single remark from Inshik. He truly was a man of few words, just as Song had said. Only now, it seemed the eyes that had once done much of his talking had lost their ability to smile. Yunmo was impatient. Still, he knew from experience that this was the kind of background digging that needed a firm yet delicate touch, like breaking off a branch from a still-green tree.

This was all the truer in this particular case, as here he was trying to get information from someone who had spent the whole day toiling in the blazing heat. The task of getting down to essentials would have to be left until after Inshik had got some food inside him. But during the meal, too, Yunmo's efforts came to nothing. When afterward Inshik lay down with his head on his wooden pillow, it looked as if he might become moderately responsive, but very soon the sum total of his contribution was a barrage of deafening snores.

Yunmo couldn't get a wink of sleep the whole night. The problem wasn't only the chorus of snores, the wheezing, and the snuffling. Though the door had been left open, the air in the room was turbid and stifling, enough to make your head swim. This was only to be expected, of course, with thirty-odd men crammed into the low, narrow room. The grinding of teeth, the exhausted sleep-muttering . . . Now and then Inshik would toss and turn, groaning as though being stretched on the rack, then swiftly fall back into his steady snoring. Though Yunmo tried every position he could think off, sleep constantly eluded him, and a dizzying phantom haunted his mind.

This must be a first for you, Mr. Reporter, but we're all used to such things here. The woman's voice rang in his ears, and he even fancied he could feel the snake coiling around his ankle.

An owl hooted somewhere close at hand, as though it were crying somewhere beneath the eaves. Eventually, Yunmo had to get up and go outside. There, the irritating whine of the grasshoppers agitated the moonlit scene.

Yunmo strolled where his feet would take him. He wandered through trees and tall grass until his whole body was damp with dew, and then, at the bottom of the potato field, he came in sight of the spring. The brilliant white of the crescent moon floated on the water's quivering surface. It occurred to Yunmo that this must be the spring where Inshik said he saw the faces of his children every morning and evening. But surely not only his children's faces? Each of those same mornings and evenings, the face of his wife must appear to him too, the woman who had begged him to work hard for the sake of their children, to work his way back to his former position!

Yunmo sat absentmindedly by the spring until his surroundings brightened with the advancing dawn. By chance, the first of the men to appear at the stream was Inshik, carrying his toothbrush in his mouth. It was clear from the look on his face how sorry he was that Yunmo's sleep had been disturbed. Was the reporter up so early because the hut had been too uncomfortable for him?

"How could I be uncomfortable?" Yunmo answered brightly. "The air is so clean and refreshing here." And his happiness wasn't feigned; this opportunity for a quiet conversation with Inshik made up for his restless night. After all, for what reason had he struggled a hundred *ri* up that mountain path only the day before, other than to see for himself how the men lived and worked in this place? To see what Inshik's strenuous efforts were all in aid of: to solve the bean paste problem for the area's inhabitants or simply to obtain a private perk? The ultimate goal of Yunmo's research had been to confirm the true character of this man Ko Inshik. So far, though, Yunmo had been thwarted at every turn.

Putting it off until some later time was not an option. It was always difficult to rock the boat, but he needed to just go for it, and there was no time like the present. Inshik had already finished brushing his teeth, and had moved on to washing his face, splashing himself with the water bubbling up from the spring.

Yunmo went straight over, sat down next to him, and plunged both hands into the water.

"Ah—it's cold!" He deliberately exaggerated his astonishment, and Inshik turned to him. "How is it, the water here? It's much colder than in the main river, no?"

"Yes, and much clearer." Puffing a few times as though to supplement this plain, straightforward answer, Inshik stood up and pulled a small towel from his waistband.

Yunmo instantly buttoned his lips, then, realizing that Inshik was not in fact about to speak, undid them again.

"Living here like this, do you think about the time when you worked in Pyongyang?" Yunmo made sure to ask this with a cheerful, almost amused tone, pulling out his handkerchief as he followed Inshik away from the spring.

"I don't have time for that. I'm new to agriculture, so I've a lot to learn. That's the only thing I've got on my mind."

"Of course. You're busy solving the town's bean paste problem."

"No, that's not what I said. . . ."

"According to Dr. Song, when you came here, Comrade Chief Technician, well, ha . . . the chief secretary even said something about a perk. . . . Do you never think about that either?"

Yunmo left the question hanging and cast a sideways glance at Inshik, wondering whether this had been overly direct. But the mild expression on the older man's face showed no change whatsoever.

"Song's talking nonsense. . . ."

"No, but it wasn't his fault. I'm the one to blame. Since whatever the business, in front of a reporter there's no way not to spill the beans."

"There are no beans to spill. Even I'm not a machine that knows nothing but work; why wouldn't I want to receive a perk and be restored to my old position? But the work I'm doing here isn't sufficient to warrant that."

Silence spun out between the two men, as the dawn breeze brought the scent of flowers in full bloom. Yunmo's face flushed as he compared Inshik's answer, which had flowed out as easily as water from a tap, with the question he'd had such difficulty formulating. That the man in front of him was capable of dissembling, of hypocrisy, was not even in the realm of possibility. If the sincerity with which Inshik devoted himself to his work were to spring from some kind of selfish motive, his hands would not have become the tough, clawed hooks they were today, and the hinge of his front gate would not have made his young children cry.

The tender morning sun was beginning to show its face through the fog that hung like a curtain above the eastern woods. Yunmo was able to polish off his article without difficulty, almost as soon as he came down from the cultivation site. But at the municipal Party meeting for joint criticism— any reporter's article naturally had to be examined by several rounds of censors, even up to the level of the provincial Party—the article was roundly rejected.

"Are individuals who deviate from the Party's leadership thereby absolved from their responsibility to work for the good of our society? If anything, those responsibilities are doubled. How on earth can someone who calls himself a reporter be so lacking in Party character?" The chief secretary's meaning was all too clear. Now that the cultivation site had begun to produce results, the municipal Party committee would take the lion's share of the credit. In its view, Ko Inshik had merely done the bidding of his superiors, and this was penance, not something that qualified him for praise.

Yunmo thought about simply abandoning the article, but the pitiful memory of Inshik's wire-threaded button continued to prey on his mind. Eventually, he decided that he had no other choice than to knuckle down, amend the article so that the praise was meted out as the Party demanded it be, and submit it to the newspaper, all the while heaping curses on the field of journalism which he had been unfortunate enough to enter. . . .

4

It was a late autumn day, a year after the article on Ko Inshik had come out in the *District Daily*. That day, when the trees that had been so abundant in summer had been reduced to gaunt skeletons, Yunmo paid a second visit to the cultivation site. Naturally, the real object of his visit was again Ko Inshik. A few days earlier, Yunmo had been passing in front of the food store in the center of town when he had overheard an exchange between two respectable women that made him stop in his tracks. Though they had simply been complaining that the times were tight indeed, with the supply of rice already being reduced every month, and with not even any bean paste to be had, Yunmo had been unable to let it just wash over him. As a journalist, he always felt a sense of commitment not only to the piece he had written, but to the individual, event, or process he had researched to write it. The bean paste problem had initially seemed to be completely solved, thanks to Inshik's cultivation site's producing two to three years' worth of raw ingredients. Now it seemed that that stockpile must have been depleted. But surely fresh supplies from the cultivation site could not have dried up completely?

Yunmo was already aware where the overarching cause lay: The situation across the country as a whole was worsening day by day, resulting in a sharp decrease in those supplies which the town received from the state; to make matters worse, storm damage—now a frequent yearly occurrence— had severely affected the output from the cultivation site. Yunmo had known this for a while, of course, but hearing his fellow townspeople dare to voice their complaints, albeit only in mutters, convinced him that he could no longer sit idly by, that he needed to go back to the cultivation site.

More than anything else, he was curious to learn how Inshik had been getting on in the meantime. How was he taking care of his children without the help of a wife? How was he taking care of himself? This year, yet again, the monsoon rains had washed the topsoil away from a considerable area of the cultivation site; how great must Inshik's dilemma be now that he was unable to provide the factory with necessary supplies, causing its production to halt completely?

Yunmo's steps quickened as he got closer to the reclaimed land. Shrikes, the "birds of autumn," searched the thickets at the side of the road for red rowan berries. When he still had a fair way to go, the top fields of the cultivation site were visible between the trees, while the view behind Yunmo showed the town spread out below like a desert waste. Deep ditches ran here and there alongside the path that led uphill—Yunmo couldn't remember them having been there before. Leaping over such a ditch, thinking that a spring shower must have rendered the fields of the reclaimed land unsuitable, he heard it: footsteps rustling on fallen leaves in the white birch forest adjacent to the path. The next moment, a man burst out from a thicket of wild grapevines. Then another, and another . . .

Each member of the group carried a heavy-looking backpack, bulging full.

"Why, aren't you the reporter?" cried a young man wearing an alpine cap. "Group leader, look, the reporter is here!"

"What?" came a voice from somewhere in the trees. On closer inspection, Yunmo could see that these were men who worked on the cultivation site. He greeted those he recognized from two years previously, reserving an especially warm greeting for Ko Inshik.

"Group leader, why don't we take this as an opportunity to have a bit of a rest?" The young man in navy leggings had a warm, friendly voice.

Swiping at the sweat on his forehead with his fist, Inshik surveyed the group. "Yes, why not?" At that, they all flopped down on the ground, still with their backpacks on. After helping Inshik take off his heavy backpack, Yunmo sat down next to him, a clump of frosted wild chrysanthemums between them. A stuffy smell rose from Inshik's sweat-soaked back and the backpack he'd removed.

Able to get a close look at him only then, Yunmo was inwardly shocked at how different Inshik looked. So different, in fact, that if it hadn't been for his distinctive thick spectacles he might genuinely have been unable to recognize him, even at this close proximity. The hair at his temples was wholly gray, and his face had been burned almost black by the sun. His hair had been black only two years ago—Yunmo found it staggering that it had turned so white.

Unbeknownst to himself, Yunmo's gaze sought out the button on Inshik's overalls. Though these were not, of course, the same pair he'd been wearing two years ago, there was one white button which stood out, the others all being black. How shabby Inshik now was, like some elderly bumpkin! For a while, the lump in Yunmo's throat was so strong he was unable to produce a single word. Eventually, though, someone addressed him.

"Hey! Are those mushrooms?" It was the young man in the alpine cap, sitting four or five paces away. "The things wrapped up in your handkerchief by your side, Mr. Reporter?"

"Oh, these? That's right, they're mushrooms. The frost has shriveled them a bit, but they're still good."

"'Good'? What are you talking about? Throw them away, at once!"

"Oh? So they aren't edible, you mean?"

"Edible or not . . . Come on, tell him what we've been through. Ah, our group leader is so close-lipped, sometimes it's like talking to a wall."

"Why do you want to tell him that awful tale?" Inshik removed his glasses and began to rub them on the front of his overalls.

"Was there some kind of accident, Comrade Chief Technician?"

"Yes, a very serious one. I heard that you were away on business at the time."

"Mr. Reporter!" the young man in blue leggings burst out impatiently, seeming agitated by the sluggishness of Inshik's speech. "One of our maids lost her life because of those mushrooms, and the rest of us could all have gone the same way!"

Yunmo was shocked.

"One of your maids? The plump one?"

"The very same. The one who hurled a snake right onto your feet!"

"Is it true, Comrade Chief Technician?"

"It's true." Inshik's voice was almost a moan. "The new maid who came to work with her didn't know the difference between mushrooms, and mixed red mushrooms into a mountain vegetable stir-fry. Ah!"

"And the other woman died? So these red mushrooms are that toxic? In that case, isn't it a stroke of luck that the rest of you didn't meet the same fate?" Yunmo looked around Inshik's group one by one.

"Yes, it was lucky. We were very ill, but we got better. There would have been a mass death otherwise."

"But if you've only just recovered from such a severe illness, why are you going around like this? With such heavy loads, that is."

"The Party has given the order to collect acorns."

"Acorns?"

"Enough to replace the harvest that's missing this year." Yunmo nodded silently, but then opened his mouth to ask, "How many kilos do you collect like this, each day?"

"We split up into six groups, and each member of a group collects twenty kilos. It's hard, but those are our orders."

At this response, Yunmo scanned the group afresh. Presumably from their wandering the rough mountainside, the white stuffing of their overalls was showing through in places. Their hands were covered in scrapes and scratches, and some had similar wounds on their faces.

Perhaps in response to Yunmo's look of sympathy, Inshik opened his mouth in self-accusation.

"It's all my fault. When the father is at fault, the children suffer too, no?"

"Group leader, that's your only fault right there," the man in the alpine hat protested, "always saying that everything is your fault! Mr. Reporter, our group leader now has to replace the soil of the reclaimed land that was washed away by the rains. The town authorities demand a harvest but won't lift a finger to help. Group leader! Do you think the rain showers are your fault, too? Well? I really don't understand why it's up to us to go hunting acorns like this."

"Dae-seok! Haven't we been through this already? Never mind where the order came from, we have to collect the acorns in order to make bean paste, as though we were doing it for our own pot."

"That's all well and good, but what about the behavior of the Party jidowon who came up here the other day? He treated you like a mere schoolboy, and in front of us all. . . ."

"Dae-seok!"

"Mr. Reporter! Listen to what I have to say, and don't think ill of me. Seeing how devoted our group leader is, we're all ready to gather acorns and improve the soil, for his sake. But those higher up have no idea how we all work ourselves to the bone here. . . ." A heavy sigh escaped from Yunmo, and the young man instantly clamped his mouth shut. He glanced in turn at Yunmo and Inshik, studying their countenances. Their tightly closed mouths, their rapidly blinking eyes . . . It was clear that his words, overly critical of the Party as they were, had made them both uncomfortable. His face stiffened. But then his attitude instantly underwent a complete change.

"But everything will turn out well in the end, group leader! And for that, I'll give you a song."

The young soybean plants
Wait only for the gentle rain
And my Chun-hyang with her cherry lips
Waits only for her young master.
Hurray! Hurray!

There was a burst of rowdy laughter. But the young man continued, keeping a straight face, "But really, group leader, who is our Chun-hyang?" From somewhere in the grass he produced a paper tobacco pouch. "She's eagerly awaiting the return of her young master, due back any day now. Me. Just like in the song."

"Dae-seok!" Inshik interrupted him. "Why don't you ask the reporter for a favor?"

"What favor?" Yunmo asked.

"A wild boar's gallbladder. His wife gave birth recently."

"Ah, really?" Yunmo turned to the young man. "I'll take it to her if it's a boy. Otherwise . . ."

"Ha, so is that a yes or a no?"

This second round of laughter flushed a mountain bird out from somewhere in the trees.

"Very well. In that case, please do give it to me." Yunmo held his hand out to the young man. "Now, Comrades, I'm prepared to help in whatever way I can in changing the soil of the reclaimed land. But that's something for later. For now, I'll be sure to deliver this package as quickly as possible. That's another way for me to help you."

"Oh, thank you . . . really, thank you," the young man said as he handed the package to Yunmo. "In fact, it was the group leader who asked an old hunter to get hold of this for my wife. Please pass that on to her as well."

"Ah! I understand. But I'll have to be able to find your house."

"That's simple enough. Down in that town where you live, have you seen something resembling a red mushroom?"

"A red mushroom? Yes, I have!"

"Mine is the house just to the rear of that building, the one that looks like a red mushroom—in other words, the municipal Party building."

"That's enough, Dae-seok!" Inshik stared at the younger man with a look of embarrassment.

"Have I said something wrong?"

"You know perfectly well. . . ."

"Ah! You mean my likening the municipal Party building to a red mushroom?"

"That's right. Why on earth would you compare that building to a horrible red mushroom?"

"Haha, think about it, Comrade Chief Technician," Yunmo put in, "the redbrick house does look a bit like a red mushroom, doesn't it?"

"Well, I suppose that now you mention it . . ."

From somewhere in the forest, a jay's uneasy cry was heard. A gust of late-autumn wind blew in gently, swaying the chrysanthemums between Yunmo and Inshik, which were still lending their beauty to the scene even after a heavy frost. As though the wind were giving those flowers the hint that a harsh winter was on its way, coming from beyond the distant mountains . . .

5

"Go on, you have a drink first."

"No, you first."

Song pushed the lid of the thermos back to Yunmo. On the newspaper spread out between them were a dish of bean paste and two slices of fresh cucumber. Song's agitation had subsided a little, and Yunmo began to urge him to waste what had already been poured; he might already have tilted the bottle to his lips too many times as it was.

"Yunmo, tell me something instead of just sighing like a pair of bellows. Is there nothing we can do?"

Yunmo made no answer. Song groaned. Only then, as though under compulsion, did Yunmo open his mouth.

"Song! What was it you said to me a little while ago?"

"When do you mean? I can't recall."

"You said that if it's a redbrick family you're going up against, better just to fold even if you hold the upper hand."

"Oh, you mean when you came about that business with your son? But why are you bringing that up now?"

"Don't misunderstand me. It's not as though I bear some grudge because you weren't able to help me out back then. You remember what it was about, though? Our Song-chol scored a hundred points in the college promotion exam, a truly magnificent score, you know. The municipal Party's organizing secretary's son got seventy-two points, but in spite of that, he was the one chosen to enter Kim Il-sung University—chosen over our son. It's taken me until now to realize that what you said back then was completely correct, a hundred times over; that even if you'd tried to help me out it would only have been in vain. So it makes me think of what you told me then. . . . Does it seem that the security services arrested your uncle on their own initiative?"

"Of course not. The decision must have come from the redbrick house."

"And still, knowing that, you want to do something about it?"

"What choice to do I have?"

Yunmo fell silent. Seeing that the other man had nothing to add, Song pulled back the thermos lid which he'd just pushed away, raised it to his mouth, and drained it to the dregs.

"Yunmo! There is something I want to tell you. There was another reason I couldn't help you out back then, and not just because it wouldn't have made any difference."

"Are you drunk already?"

"No, listen. I'm talking about an accusation, a denunciation. For your ears only."

"A denunciation!"

"Listen. . . . I was well aware why you chose me to visit that day. Not so much to make use of my influence, exactly, but because you hoped I'd put in a good word with someone higher up. You know who I'm talking about, don't you? The chief secretary's wife. It's an open secret that I'm a favorite of hers, the woman known throughout the province as 'Chief Secretary No. 2.' For whatever reason, this woman took an interest in me, even down to finding a position for my wife, just because I was a favorite of hers. This was perfectly clear, even to outsiders. Outsiders like you, who thought that if they got me on their side, the chief secretary could be set against the organizing secretary. Am I right?"

"Well, and what of it?"

"What you didn't know was that at the time, I'd already fallen from her good graces. You have no idea, I'm telling you. It's a dirty business. . . ."

"Indeed! So things had gone wrong for you?"

"I was heading home after work one day when I got a phone call from 'Chief Secretary No. 2' begging for a house call. I went. I rang the bell, she came out in person to open the gate for me, then walked back in and lay down on the bed. A splendid double bed. I'd made plenty of house calls on the chief secretary himself, but still I hung back. Granted, she was ten years my senior, but even so, the thought of the two of us alone in her bedroom troubled me. Then she starts up complaining about how dreary her life is, with her husband's having been summoned yet again to the Party's provincial committee to respond to complaints regarding the bean paste supply, and her son away at a military encampment, making me understand that we were alone in the house. I saw through the reason for this seemingly inane chatter—she wanted to let me know that the two of us were the only ones in the house. She was clearly suggesting something."

"Hang on—the chief secretary had been summoned to the provincial committee because of the bean paste issue?"

"That was actually the second time, though of course you wouldn't have known."

"Twice, to the provincial committee! So it was as big an issue as that. . . ."

"This is why you need to listen to my story first. Whatever the woman was getting at, I needed to do my duty as a doctor, so I began to open up my house call bag. She offered me a cigarette, saying I could probably do with one, what with her making me come over in such a rush. She picked up a pack of high-quality cigarettes from her bedside, as though they had been placed there deliberately in advance, and held it out to me.

"I declined politely, and began to question her about her condition. She told me that her stomach had been somewhat upset since lunch, and though I hadn't yet asked her to, she slipped off her blouse, and even pushed down her underskirt a little. She was flaunting her taut breasts and white stomach; no doubt it was the abundance of flesh that had helped them retain a smooth, youthful appearance. I began to examine her with my stethoscope, but could detect nothing untoward. I examined her again by percussion, but the result was the same.

"So I began to put pressure on her internal organs, when she suddenly grasped my wrist with both of her hands, coiled an arm around my waist, and pulled me to her, panting out, 'Oh Dr. Song, oh Dr. Song.' I recoiled, shook her off as though she were a caterpillar clinging to my body, and took a step back. At that, she dropped the show. Why had I pulled back? she wanted to know. Because I was afraid of her husband? There was no need. I had no need to worry about that old man, who had eyes only for young girls.

"She panted my name again. With no time to think it through, I fled the room. I banged the gate closed, stethoscope still in hand, then was forced to bend over where I was and spit on the ground. It was her impudence, her haughtiness, even more than her animal lust that made me feel dirtied. Just because she was the wife of a high-up functionary at the redbrick house, she thought she could bend the whole world to her desires, as though she were God. Yunmo! Would I have been able to speak these shameful words to anyone else? So you see, when you came to see me about your son, I was busy dealing with that shame, alone. . . . I was convinced I had only a few days left before being dismissed from my post as doctor."

Yunmo abruptly roared with laughter. Song's eyes goggled in surprise.

"So what you're saying is, as long as she's from the redbrick house, a woman can make anyone her 'comfort man'?"

"Leave off. I didn't become her sex slave."

"The redbrick house! That beats everything." Yunmo pressed his hand over his heart. "How foolish I was when I came to see you then. Such a fool!"

"But haven't I come to see you now on just such a fool's errand? In fact, this fire burning inside me . . . I can't put it out. . . ."

"Song! Restrain yourself. Things are already in motion. What good does it do to keep tormenting yourself? Here, look at this!" Yunmo picked up the notepad from his desk and held it out for Song to see.

"What is it?"

"Don't you have eyes in your head? The bean paste factory of N Town returns to normal production."

"You're nickname's already 'Mr. Bullshit Reporter'; are you really going to tarnish your reputation further by writing such nonsense?"

"But it's true that, right now, bean paste is fermenting in the factory's tanks. The redbrick house cooked up a scheme to make use of livestock feed for it. Since the factory's chief technician, who was the direct cause of the shortage, has been removed, bean paste will have to pour out for all the people of the area to see, no? They have to prove that it wasn't the Party's mistake, that it was all the fault of the workers, you see?"

"I see. So that's how things stand, is it?"

"Right. I only just realized it myself, hearing you say that the chief secretary had twice been summoned to appear in front of the provincial Party committee. The crow flies, and the pear falls, as they say; that's exactly what's happened to your uncle!"

"You're right—it's obvious."

"So now where can we take our complaint to? The general court? The legal department of the Administrative Committee? Ha! Constitution, administration, legislation—we both know the redbrick house has all levels of the law tight in its fist."

"Ah! Why did I ever hang this around my neck?" Song exploded, madly agitated, striking his side where the pocket containing his Party membership card was. "Why did I become a lady-in-waiting at the brick house, of my own accord?"

"Because you were deceived by a mask, a front, like me. Deceived by those slogans—'Equality'; 'Democracy'; 'The

People Are the Masters of History'—the ones that looked nice enough on the surface, but had the knife of dictatorship underneath."

"You're right. In all of creation, the rule is that the more toxic something is, the more pretty and friendly it's made to look."

"That's the truth. Like poisonous mushrooms!"

"Ah, it's too much! How can we be sitting on our hands like this, when an innocent man is being brought to harm right in front of our eyes?"

Song snatched at his clothes and tore the buttons off in a scatter. The image of Ko Inshik, who would at that moment be sitting in a cell in handcuffs, rose into Yunmo's mind, and he hurled himself indignantly from his seat. He opened the curtains and struggled to blink back the tears as he gazed in the direction of the security services prison.

Dark inky clouds were veiling the sky—a storm might have been coming. The curtain fluttered in the strong wind, threatening to tear.

6

The hearing regarding Ko Inshik took place in a public sports ground at the foot of the mountain. From early in the morning, a steady stream of people began to file across the Seongcheon Bridge and into the stadium: a mix of officials, factory employees, and ordinary citizens. Similar crowds were always organized for such events.

Once ten o'clock came around, the judges filed out and took their seats on the specially erected podium. Up until then, the handcuffed Inshik had been made to stand by the vehicle used for transporting criminals, which had been parked to the rear of the podium; now, several security officers dragged him up next to the platform. Presently, the prosecution statement began to be read out. It was not particularly long.

> In these difficult times, when the situation of provisions across the country is worsening owing to a cold front of weather, the establishment of a cultivation site to provide the soybean factory with raw ingredients was a matter of significance for the entire town. The municipal Party committee entrusted this task to Ko Inshik. In the early days of his carrying out these duties, Ko Inshik worked with such diligence that his name even appeared in the newspaper. However, his neglect of and irresponsibility toward his work has since become gradually apparent, as has the fact that his initial efforts were a hypocritical attempt to wipe his records clean. No measures whatsoever were put in place to cope with the storms which return each year, and ninety thousand *pyeong* of the cultivation site has recently been almost completely ruined. As a consequence, the soybean factory's supply of raw ingredients was cut off, and the citizens of our town have been unable to receive their bean paste rations. Moreover, as the individual in question had hidden himself comfortably away at the cultivation site, the

duties he ought to have been overseeing at the factory, including the development of new technologies, have been left to stagnate. The accused has been living in his "sweet kingdom" in the mountains, out of reach of the Party's control, where his inability to manage even his own men ultimately led to an incident in which one revolutionary comrade died from eating poisonous mushrooms.

What cannot be overlooked is that, despite being sent down from Pyongyang for falsifying his family history, the accused failed to reward the Party's trust, amply demonstrated by their assigning this extremely important position to an individual with such a record. Rather than displaying the greatest loyalty, which would have been the only appropriate response, the accused in fact harbored discontent and committed the crimes detailed above, thus bringing about hardships for our people which still cause the Party such pain to witness. For that reason, the punishment must be still more severe.

This was the full content of the prosecution statement. There was no defense. Any defense of an antirevolutionary element who had disturbed the tranquillity of the people would itself stand accused, next to the man it had defended. The crowd was perfectly familiar with the way judgments were passed in this country—no one expected a defense.

Seated on the podium, the chief judge turned to Ko In-shik and began his questions.

"Accused! Do you acknowledge the charges brought against you, Ko Inshik?"

The crowd's collective gaze shifted to Inshik like the mass surge of a swelling tide. The look on his face just then! His lips twitched soundlessly like those of an idiot, while his eyes stared blankly over the heads of the crowd, in the direction of the town's central streets. But none could know the exact spot on which his gaze had landed: the municipal Party office—the red mushroom.

"He seems to have lost his senses!" A fluttering swell rose in the stadium, then subsided, like the shiftings of the nighttime sea, an instant later.

"Silence! Accused, are you listening?" No reply.

In spite of his efforts at self-control, Yunmo felt a rasping sound from inside himself push at his tightly closed lips. What answer could Ko Inshik make now? From those early days reclaiming the land, when his eyes had watered at the half-burned charcoal which was all he'd had to use by way of kindling; when he'd injured his hands by pulling up tree roots and rolling rocks away; that early morning when, with a heavy heart, he'd gone in pursuit of the wild boar, picturing the incense sticks his children would be lighting on their mother's offertory table; that later morning when he'd had a narrow escape from death, opening his eyes on his wooden pillow after being struck down by poisonous mushrooms; those days and days on end when he'd gone out to gather acorns and replace the soil that had been washed away—on

all such days, without fail, he had cultivated flowers of conscience unselfishly in his heart!

Those flowers had now been struck by a bolt of lightning,
in broad daylight, flattening all their stems—how could Inshik
now hope to make them stand upright? He would be lucky
if his heart didn't burst in his chest, causing him to faint in
the face of such injustice!

Those who were sitting as close to Inshik as Yunmo was
were able to hear him muttering, "*There's* one, *there's* one,"
jerking his cuffed hands for all the world as though he were
trying to uproot a weed. Then, seeming pleased at having
accomplished some task, he tipped his head back to face the
sky and let out a thrilling laugh.

Amplified by the microphone in front of him, that laughter boomed through the stadium, striking a chill into the
hearts of the audience. They regarded Ko Inshik more closely,
and found that the expression on his face had altered. That
face was now frozen rigid, belying the laughter that had just
burst from it. Inshik stretched his cuffed hands out in front of
him as though trying to grasp something. This time, his voice
was neither loud nor soft, a muttering that was also a scream.

"There it is . . . still there! Please go and pull up that
red mushroom. That terrible thing— there! Please, can you
hear me?"

The crowd stirred again, and someone on the podium
rapped on a table to call for silence.

"What's happened to him?"

"He must have gone soft in the head."

"What's that he said about a red mushroom? What's he talking about?"

But there was no one in the stadium who could guess what Inshik meant, aside from Yunmo and a couple of Inshik's fellow workers from the cultivation site. The voice of Inshik scolding the young man in the alpine cap, who had likened the municipal Party office to a ghastly red mushroom, rang out clearly in Yunmo's ears.

Red mushroom! For Yunmo, those two simple words, though the product of a deranged mind, told of the hundreds and thousands of other words that must have been boiling inside Inshik at that very moment, consuming him like the fires of hell.

Now that Inshik's snow-white conscience had finally recognized the poisonous mushroom that had put down roots in this land, he was summoning a desperate strength to pull it up from the ground, that mushroom stained with deceit and oppression, with tyranny and pacification.

The announcer went up to the microphone.

"You are hereby informed that owing to the accused's apparently no longer being in possession of all his faculties, today's trial is adjourned." The announcer's voice was still coming from the speakers when a roiling cry broke from among the crowd.

"Father!"

Inshik's son and daughter pushed their way through to the front of the crowd in a mad flurry. Song, who had been sitting with them, had tried to restrain them, but in vain. The crowd, who had stood up to leave, all sat down again.

Yet though their father was right there in front of them, the two children still were denied their reunion. Struggling along behind the car for transporting criminals, choking in the black exhaust fumes it was spewing out, the children called helplessly for their father, their voices going to the hearts of those who were watching.

When the crowd had dispersed, one person was left standing beneath the white poplar at the front of the otherwise deserted stadium, a handkerchief clutched in his hand. Yunmo. The tears he had held back while in front of others could no longer be restrained. He cried for Ko Inshik, a man who had sacrificed everything he had, and been rewarded by having even hope taken away from him.

Yunmo's gaze was directed squarely at the municipal Party office—the red mushroom—which Inshik had clearly been staring at over the heads of the crowd. How many noble lives had been lost to its poison! The root of all human misfortune and suffering was that red European specter that the lion-headed man with the tobacco pipe had boasted had put down roots in this land, the seed of that red mushroom!

Yunmo clenched his fists with crushing strength, unable to tear his gaze from the so-called redbrick house, his heart ringing with the gruesome cry which Ko Inshik had been unable to speak.

Pull out that red mushroom, that poisonous mushroom. Uproot it from this land, from this world, forever!

3rd July, 1993

Afterword

How *The Accusation* Came Out of North Korea
Kim Seong-dong, writer for the *Monthly Chosun*

The South Korean publication of this piece of fiction, which sharply criticizes and satirizes the North Korean regime, and which is written by a man who still lives and works under that same system, is a historical first—nothing like it has emerged in the sixty-eight years since the peninsula was divided. Though memoirs and pieces of fiction by North Korean defectors, of a similarly critical tone, have indeed been published now and then, these have all been written after their authors' escape to the free world. No work denouncing the oppressive, antidemocratic regime of North Korea, by a writer still living in North Korea, has ever before been published.

As a manuscript, *The Accusation* consisted of seven hundred and fifty sheets of paper, each holding two hundred characters. The indentations made by the pressure of the writer's pencil are plainly visible, while the faded paper indicates the long gestation of the work. It is a collection of short stories, seven in total. Though each treats a different incident, with its own distinct cast of characters, the collection can be thought of as an omnibus, the stories yoked together to one overarching theme—criticism of the Kim Il-sung era.

Each time we come to the end of an individual story, we find a date—"1997.7.3," for example, written in the Korean fashion with the month preceding the day. We presume that these indicate the date at which the writer completed a given story. "Record of a Defection," which comes first according to this chronology, is dated December 1989.

Chronologically, the last story in this collection is "Pandemonium." This story, which strips away the trappings of benevolence to reveal the brutality of Kim Il-sung's dictatorship, is dated December 1995; it was completed after the death of the self-styled Great Leader. Thus, we can see that Bandi has for a long time been writing fiction criticizing the North Korean regime, which has changed hands from Kim Il-sung to Kim Jong-il, and from Kim Jong-il to Kim Jong-un, whose rule Bandi is currently living under.

Bandi is a member of the Chosun Writers' League Central Committee, North Korea's state-authorized writers' association.*

* Biographical details have been altered in order to protect the identity of Bandi.

North Korea's most significant instrument of control over the arts, literature as well as fine art, is the Chosun Workers' Party Department of Propaganda and Agitation, of which Kim Jong-il was made director around the time of his being named successor. Writers, for whom affiliation with the Chosun Literature and Art General League is obligatory, receive guidance on suitable topics from the Department of Propaganda and Agitation, a department that also censors their work. The Chosun Writers' League Central Committee is a literature-specific subsidiary organization of the Chosun Literature and Art General League.

This tightly controlled system means that literary talent is far from the only criterion for becoming a writer in North Korea. As with all prestigious positions there, the most important considerations are family background and social standing. Opportunities for getting work published are few and far between, and there is only a small amount of space allotted for literature in newspapers and magazines, affording those writers who do manage to publish particularly high status.

Kim Sung-min, who now works at the Seoul-based Free North Korea Radio, made his South Korean literary debut by publishing twelve poems in 2004; before defecting, he had been active as a poet and playwright in his native North Korea, where he was also a member of the Chosun Literature and Art General League. The defector Jang Jin-sung, who came to prominence with his 2008 poetry collection *Selling My Daughter for One Hundred Won*, was another.

In North Korea, the traditional path to becoming a writer involves having one's work published in a centrally issued newspaper or magazine. Bandi himself trod this path.

He was born in a northeastern province of the Korean Peninsula, Hamgyeong, which is bordered to the north by China and Russia. He was a child when the Korean War broke out, the war which South Korea refers to by the date of its beginning, 6.25, and which the North has dubbed the "Fatherland Liberation War." Having gravitated toward literature from a young age, Bandi was in his twenties when he first saw his writing published in North Korean magazines and began to make a name for himself.

All the same, he tried to put the dream of a writing career aside, choosing instead to live among the workers. But literature refused to relinquish its hold on him, and he wrote stories and poems in whatever spare moments he could find. His talent was simply too great to remain undiscovered. Spurred on by recognition and encouragement from those close to him, he joined the Chosun Literature and Art General League, and soon became a regular contributor to its various periodicals.

And yet, something began to weigh on him: the great famine of the early to mid-1990s, exacerbated by floods but stemming from the disastrous economic policies of previous decades, which the government insisted on referring to by the officially mandated code words "the Arduous March." Witnessing scenes of misery and deprivation, in which many of his friends and colleagues perished, provoked him to reflect deeply on the society in which he lived, and his role there as a writer. A writer's strength, he found, is best deployed within writing. And so he began to record the lives of those whom hunger and social contradictions had brought to an untimely death, or who had been forced to leave their homes and roam the countryside in search of food. Now, when Bandi picked up his pencil, he did so in order to denounce the system.

In this, Bandi took upon himself the role of a spokesperson denouncing the misery inflicted on the North Korean people by North Korean–style socialism, a system riddled with internal contradictions in which individuals were classified according to a social standing determined at birth and could be condemned as guilty by association. One by one, he collected instances in which citizens were forced to swallow this painful reality, without being able to breathe a word of complaint, and threaded them into his stories. These stories each described and denounced a real situation, which can be difficult to combine with literary excellence; but Bandi considered it his duty as a writer to produce work whose literariness would, in a sense, live up to the reality of the events he described. Needless to say, it was a long and difficult process.

As time went by these stories and poems gradually built up into a sizable body of work, yet their readership was always limited to a single person—Bandi himself. Even before he picked up his pencil, Bandi would have been aware that, in his society, no other situation was possible. Yet still he carried on writing, in patient hope of a time when things would be different, when his denunciation of the North Korean system might circulate freely in the world outside its borders. The realization of this dream was set in motion by the defection of one of his close relatives. The manuscript's journey is detailed below, and is based on the testimony of Do Hee-yun, representative of the Citizens' Coalition for Human Rights of Abductees and North Korean Refugees, into whose hands it came.

On an otherwise ordinary day, one of Bandi's relatives came to call on him. Broaching the subject cautiously, she let him know that in three days' time she would attempt to flee to China. Bandi had himself considered defecting, but thoughts of his wife and children had always held him back. Now, he saw his relative's planned escape as an excellent opportunity to make his writing known abroad. He described his works to her, judging that it would be safe to reveal their dissident nature to someone who intended to flee the country, someone to whom he was close enough to trust.

Into the hands of this woman, who intended to escape from North Korea entirely alone, he pressed a manuscript of stories and poems criticizing the system under which they had both suffered. But since there was no guarantee that her escape would be successful, and they could not risk having the manuscript fall into the hands of the North Korean border police, she went back home that day empty-handed, promising to send for the manuscript once the route for her escape was set.

Once again, Bandi had to hide his work—work that he was determined would someday be seen—in some deep, dark place. Several months went by.

Though his relative escaped over the border to China, she did not get far before being picked up by a group of Chinese soldiers. Luckily, these soldiers took note of her smart appearance, so different from that of the other defectors they'd encountered, and deduced that she was from a high-ranking family. Rather than sending her back over the border, they demanded a bribe of 10 million North Korean won, or 50,000 yuan (around $7,500).

Explaining that she didn't carry such large amounts with her, the woman asked to be allowed to contact various people who might be able to get the money together for her. While this negotiation was going on, the unit commander went to Yanji, where he met up with a man he'd heard of, a blogger who wrote about North Korean refugees. The commander informed the blogger that a female defector was being held by his unit, and asked him to inquire about her connections, as his and his men's intention was to release her once they had received the bribe money.

As it turned out, this blogger was an old acquaintance of Representative Do Hee-yun. Learning of the situation, Representative Do immediately turned his attentions to rescuing the woman, Bandi's relative, from being sent back to North Korea. But the considerable expense involved was a problem; it was enough of a struggle for Representative Do to scrape together the funds needed to run his human rights organization. After racking his brains for some time, he called on a man who had occasionally donated to his cause, and explained the situation to him. The man loaned him the 10 million won, asking that it be paid back later if everything turned out as hoped. With this money as a bribe, Representative Do was able to secure the woman's release and arrange for her to be brought from China to South Korea. In this way, Representative Do became a part of the writer Bandi's story.

But the connection did not happen immediately. Once the woman had been formally admitted to the Republic of Korea and sent to the Settlement Support Center for North Korean Refugees, Representative Do promptly forgot all about her. She was, after all, only one of many defectors whom he had helped, and who very rarely got in touch with him after being discharged from the Support Center.

This time was different. After she left the Support Center, the woman contacted Representative Do several times, on her own initiative, eventually arranging for him to visit her in her new home, situated in one of Seoul's satellite cities. There, she presented Representative Do with an envelope of money, explaining that this was the only way she had of expressing her gratitude. Representative Do refused to accept the envelope, knowing that what she was offering him was a part of the resettlement funds which she had been given to use while she found her feet in a new country.

But the woman's stubbornness was equal to Representative Do's. She asked him to do a favor for her, and to take the envelope as the fee to cover this. When Representative Do asked what kind of a favor she had in mind, the name "Bandi" came up. The woman said, "If I'd fled the country with that manuscript in my possession, the soldiers would have found it and both Bandi and I would now be dead," and "I promised him I would get it out somehow, so he will be waiting." The woman also explained in detail just how prominent a state writer Bandi was.

Representative Do found himself seized by a strange feeling, a premonition that the opportunity being presented him was one that was unlikely to come again. The woman wrote a letter, which she asked Representative Do to pass on to Bandi. He would trust whoever carried that letter, she said, enough to give that person his precious manuscript.

As he left the woman's house, carrying both the letter and the envelope of money, Representative Do decided that he needed to at least give it a try. But this was no simple task. At that time, the situation at the border was thorny, and it would not be easy to find someone who would be able to travel unmolested all the way to where Bandi was living.

And in fact, the plan might not have come off at all if it hadn't been for one of those remarkable coincidences that sometimes come about in life. A Chinese friend of Representative Do informed Do that he was going to pay a visit to one of his North Korean relatives, who just so happened to live in the same small city where Bandi, thanks to his social status, also had his home. The Chinese friend assured Representative Do that he would be able to call on Bandi, too, during a meal or break time, and make the visit short enough that it wouldn't attract attention. Representative Do agreed to the plan, but warned his friend that he ought to disguise Bandi's manuscript by sandwiching it between North Korean propaganda books such as *The Selected Works of Kim Il-sung* or *The Legacy of Works by Kim Jong-il*.

Several months after his relative's successful defection, then, Bandi received a visit from Representative Do's Chinese friend, who gave him the letter wrapped in a plastic bag.

After reading the letter carefully, Bandi appeared lost in thought. He seemed to be hesitating over whether or not to trust this messenger, but after a while he went off to fetch the manuscript bundle from its hiding place. Later on, the Chinese man described the look on Bandi's face as he'd handed the manuscript over as that of a man compelled to act as he did, "as though it made no difference whether he died like this or like that."

And so the manuscript traveled via China to reach Representative Do, concealed by *The Selected Works of Kim Il-sung*.

At the time of this writing, over 28,000 North Korean defectors have entered South Korea. A great many of these have since written books—memoirs, poetry, and occasionally some fiction—criticizing North Korean society and its bankrupt system of hereditary dictatorship. Twenty-eight are members of a subsidiary of PEN International, the North Korean Writers in Exile PEN Center, which was formed at a general meeting of the parent organization in 2012.

At the 78th PEN International literary forum, held in September 2012 in the South Korean city of Gyeongju, Do Myung-hak spoke of his experience writing poetry in North Korea.

"I wanted to write poems filled with truth, poems that I myself truly felt impelled to write. In August 2004 I was arrested by a Bowibu [secret police] officer and taken deep into the Chagangdo Mountains. My satirical poems, which I had written purely to gain comfort from the act of giving literary expression to such thoughts, aware that they could never be published in North Korea, were condemned as reactionary. In prison, the guards kicked me with their combat boots until I was half dead. Sleep became impossible for me."

Do Myung-hak suffered this agony, too great to be imagined by those in the civilized world, merely for writing satirical poetry; Bandi's work goes beyond satire—it is close to a direct denunciation of the North Korean system. On top of this, after Kim Il-sung's death in 1994, Kim Jong-il instructed the North Korean literati to produce "Great Leader Eternal Life Literature," and poetry cherishing the memory of Kim Il-sung began to pour out. But even in such a period, the writer Bandi filled his literature with ridicule and denunciation of Kim Il-sung.

These were works that could not be written without risking one's life. Risking one's life to resist a system of oppression can be interpreted as having a premonition of that system's end. In this sense, the literature produced by resistance writers who live within North Korea, exposing the face of the nation to the world, is in itself the beginning of an epoch-making upheaval, showing that cracks are now appearing in the hereditary dictatorship, which has seemed until now an impregnable fortress.

The South Korean publication of Bandi's story collection criticizing the North Korean system recalls the case of Aleksandr Solzhenitsyn, who was banished from the USSR for criticizing the communist system in work which was published abroad, and who was awarded the Nobel Prize in 1970. Solzhenitsyn voluntarily enrolled as an artillery officer after the outbreak of the Second World War, and sent a letter to a friend criticizing Stalin. When this was discovered, in 1945, Solzhenitsyn was arrested, and he spent the next eight years in exile, including time in a forced labor camp. After being "rehabilitated" in 1957, he began to write *One Day in the Life of Ivan Denisovich*, based on his experiences during those eight years of banishment, and when it was published in a Russian literary magazine in 1962 he became known around the world.

His maiden work was his representative work, however, as the antiestablishment inclination of each subsequent work blocked the route to uncensored publication within the USSR itself. In protest, Solzhenitsyn sent a letter to the 1967 Soviet Writers' Congress calling for the abolition of censorship. Ultimately, this frustration led to his publishing *Cancer Ward* abroad, and this proved to be an important work in the decision of the Nobel Committee. Once his works were available abroad, the Soviet Writers' Union struck Solzhenitsyn from its membership in 1969.

The overseas publication of *The Gulag Archipelago*, which exposed the inner workings of the Soviet forced labor camps and became his other representative work, led to Solzhenitsyn's being forcibly banished from his home country, the USSR, in 1974.

For a writer, the loss of the motherland can be as grave a wound as death. But though they share the unhappy experience of having their most important work published only in a country that is not their own, Solzhenitsyn appears to have fared better than Bandi, who has to risk his life in order to write. Solzhenitsyn was able to write under his own name, with everything aboveboard, and to have some of the work which bore his name, and which criticized the system he himself suffered under, published at home, but the situation which Bandi is faced with does not allow for this.

Rather than himself trying to escape from North Korea, the writer Bandi has sent his work out as an envoy, risking his life in the process. Surely this is because he believes that external efforts can transform the slave society he lives in more quickly than internal ones. On handing his manuscript over, Bandi said that even if his work was published only in South Korea, that would be enough for him. This work should be heard as an earnest entreaty to shine a spotlight on North Korea's oppressive regime.

A Note from Do Hee-yun

Representative of the Citizens' Coalition for Human Rights
of Abductees and North Korean Refugees

B andi was born in 1950. He followed his parents to China
to take refuge there during the Korean War. He spent his
youth in China, before returning to North Korea, where he
became affiliated with the Chosun Writers' League Central
Committee. Having always shown a predisposition toward
literature, Bandi came to prominence in the 1970s, as his
work was published in North Korean magazines.

The focus of Bandi's writing changed forever after the
deaths of many people close to him during the so-called Arduous March, which began with the death of Kim Il-sung in 1994.
The experiences of this time, including seeing many North
Koreans leave their homeland just in order to survive, made
him resolve to share with the outside world a true likeness

of North Korean society as he himself saw it. Though life in North Korea was lived behind an iron curtain, Bandi held fast to the belief that his writing would have its day, and had produced a considerable body of work by the time a relative living in Hamheung province came in secret to see him and disclosed her decision to try to escape from the country by crossing over to China. Bandi was aware that he could not try to escape himself, for he had a wife and children, but three days later, when his relative left, he gave her the manuscript he had in his possession.

The relative who accepted the task of smuggling out the manuscript explained to him that, as there was no guarantee she herself would be able to get away safely, she would prepare her escape route and then return to collect it. Making this promise, she left.

Though disheartened, Bandi had no other option. Several months later, an unfamiliar youth came to his house and, without saying a word, handed him a letter wrapped in a plastic bag. The content of the letter was as follows:

> It's Myung-ok. I'm sorry this is late. I've come to a convenient place now. The one who helped me make it here safely will send someone to you. With my letter. When you get it, please give them the item which you gave to me last time. You can trust them. Since it's something that only you and I know about, there were two items which you gave to me that time, you know. Since you will also have to try living in a good

world one time, when you think of the family you left behind you will shed only tears. Such a day will surely come. Dear one, you and I will surely meet again . . .

In the meantime, stay well.

Myung–ok.

Bandi hesitated for a moment before fetching the manuscript from out of the small cupboard in which he had hidden it and handing it over to the young man, putting his trust in the letter. The young man accepted the package and immediately left the house. The manuscript that had been in Bandi's possession was now going to South Korea, to a land of freedom and hope.

And now *The Accusation* is now going out into the world to illuminate the darkness which shrouds North Korea, just like a beautiful firefly, the pen name this writer chose for himself.

In Place of Acknowledgments

[An untitled poem included with the manuscript
of *The Accusation*]

Fifty years in this northern land
Living as a machine that speaks
Living as a human under a yoke
Without talent
With a pure indignation
Written not with pen and ink
But with bones drenched with blood and tears
Is this writing of mine

Though they be dry as a desert
And rough as a grassland
Shabby as an invalid
And primitive as stone tools
Reader!
I beg you to read my words.

—Bandi